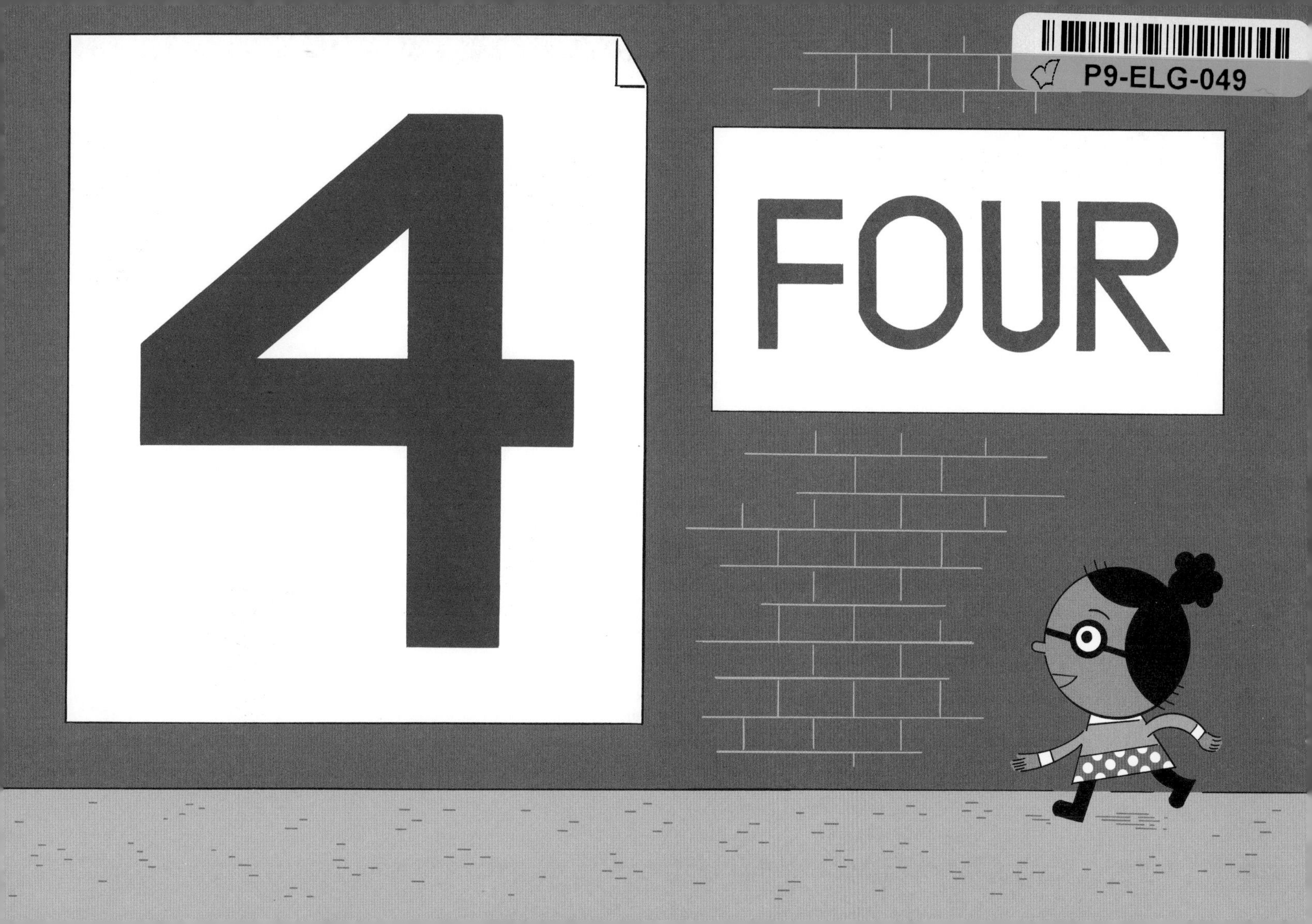
4
FOUR

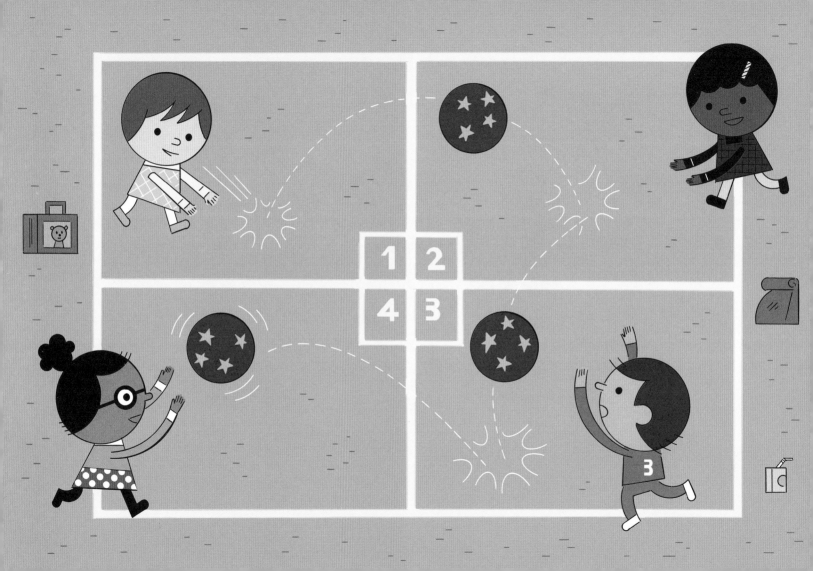

# THREE TIMES FOUR

# 3×4

## WITH ANNEMARIE

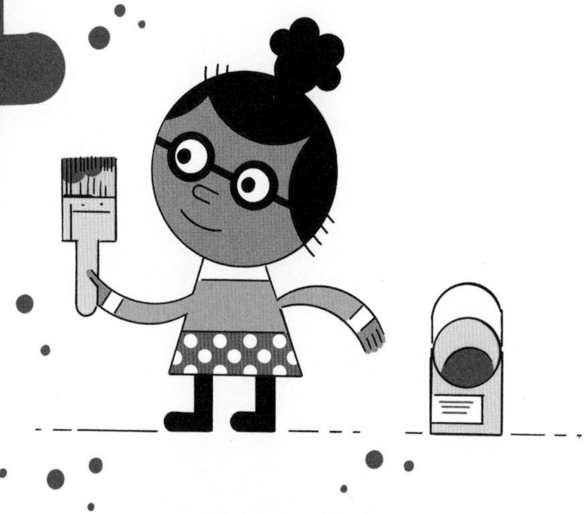

A TOON BOOK BY

ivan brunetti

# A 2019 MATHICAL HONOR BOOK

Also look for **WORDPLAY**, by the same author

## For Laura

Editorial Director: FRANÇOISE MOULY

Book Design: IVAN BRUNETTI & FRANÇOISE MOULY

IVAN BRUNETTI'S artwork was done in India ink and colored digitally.

A TOON Book™ © 2018 Ivan Brunetti & TOON Books, an imprint of Raw Junior, LLC, 27 Greene Street, New York, NY 10013. No part of this book may be used or reproduced in any manner whatsoever without written permission except in the case of brief quotations embodied in critical articles and reviews. TOON Graphics™, TOON Books®, LITTLE LIT® and TOON Into Reading!™ are trademarks of RAW Junior, LLC. All rights reserved. Library of Congress Cataloging-in-Publication Data: Names: Brunetti, Ivan, author, illustrator. Title: 3x4 : a TOON book / by Ivan Brunetti. Other titles: Three times four  Description: New York, NY : TOON Books, 2018. | Summary: Annemarie and eleven other classmates find various ways to draw sets of twelve and learn about multiplication along the way.  Identifiers: LCCN 2018000544 | ISBN 9781943145348  Subjects: LCSH: Graphic novels. | CYAC: Graphic novels. |  Multiplication--Fiction.  Classification: LCC PZ7.7.B813 Aah 2018 | DDC 741.5/973--dc23  LC record available at https://lccn.loc.gov/2018000544   All our books are Smyth Sewn (the highest library-quality binding available) and printed with soy-based inks on acid-free, woodfree paper harvested from responsible sources. Printed in China by C&C Offset Printing Co., Ltd. Distributed to the trade by Consortium Book Sales & Distribution, a division of Ingram Content Group; orders (866) 400-5351; ips@ingramcontent.com; www.cbsd.com

ISBN: 978-1-943145-34-8 (hardcover)

19 20 21 22 23 24 C&C 10 9 8 7 6 5 4 3 2

WWW.TOON-BOOKS.COM

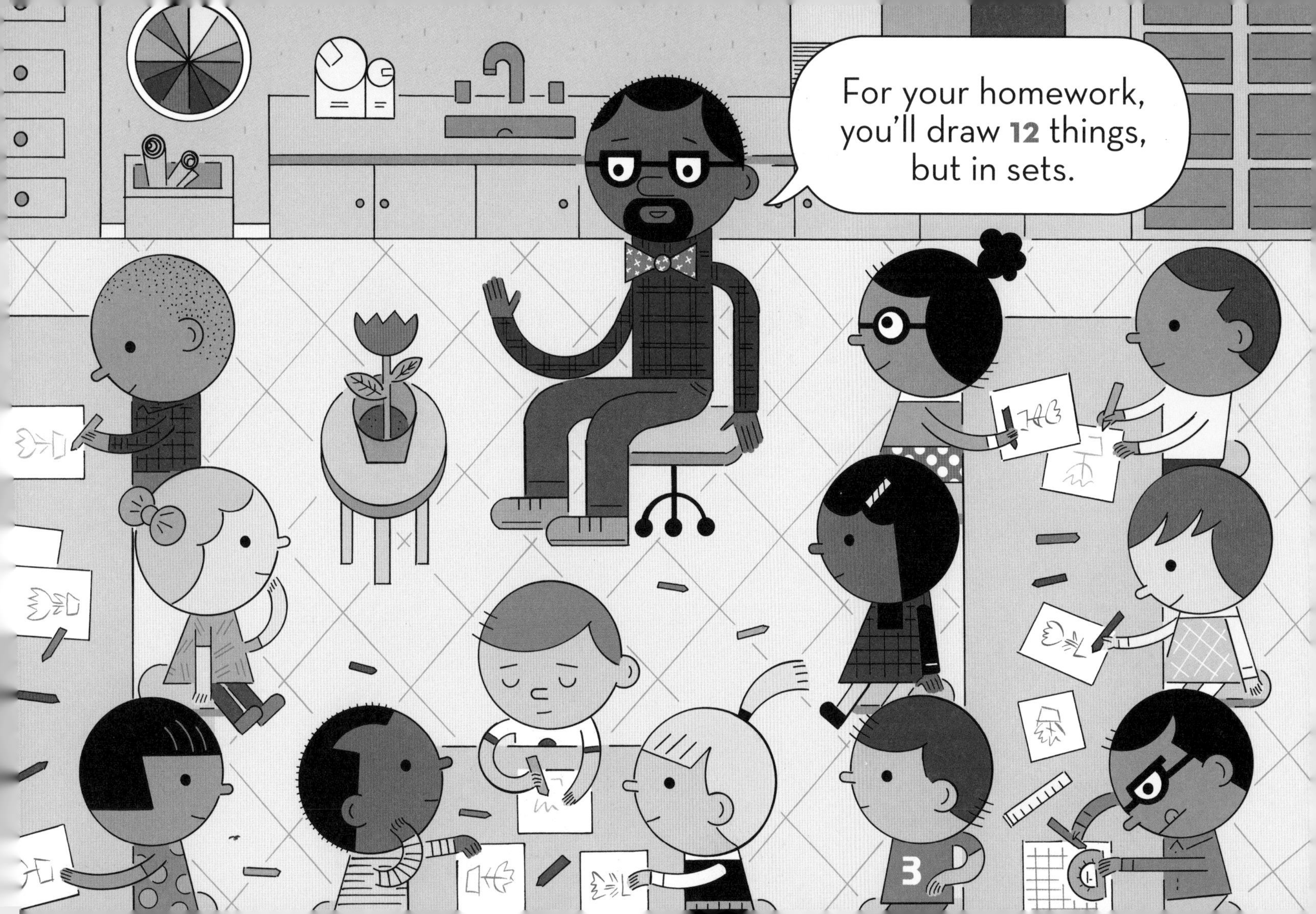
For your homework, you'll draw **12** things, but in sets.
3

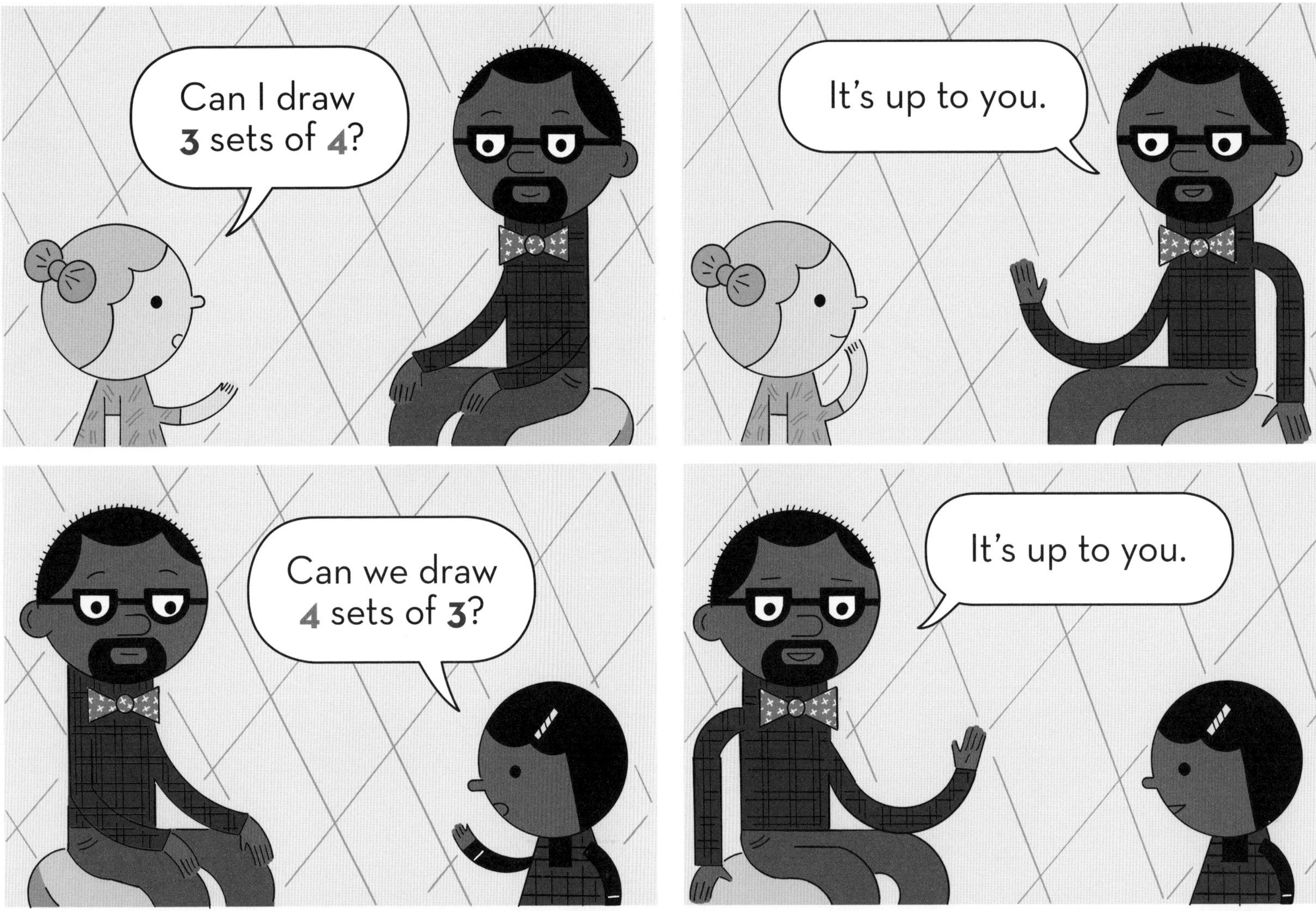
Can I draw 3 sets of 4?
It's up to you.
Can we draw 4 sets of 3?
It's up to you.

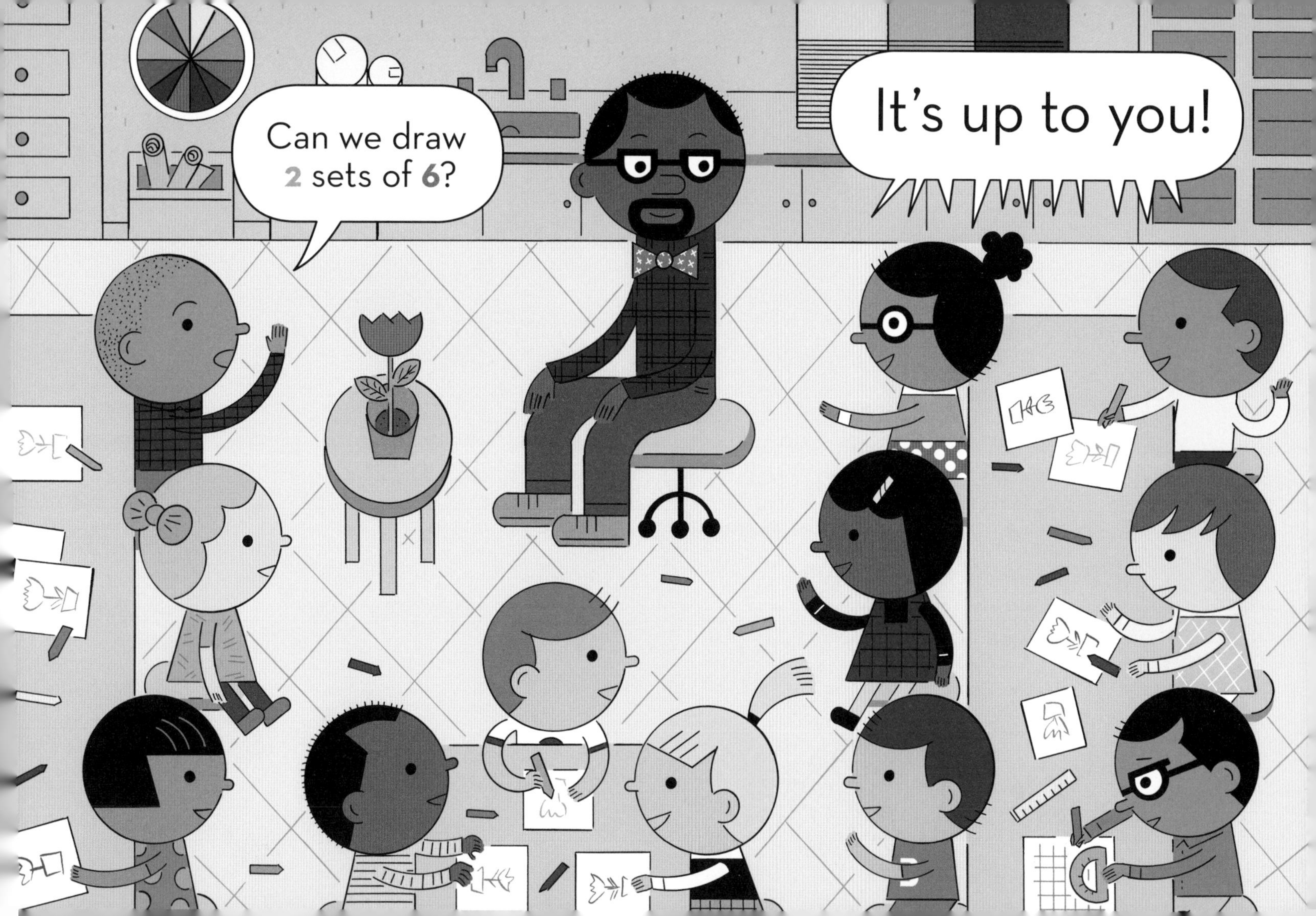
Can we draw 2 sets of 6?
It's up to you!

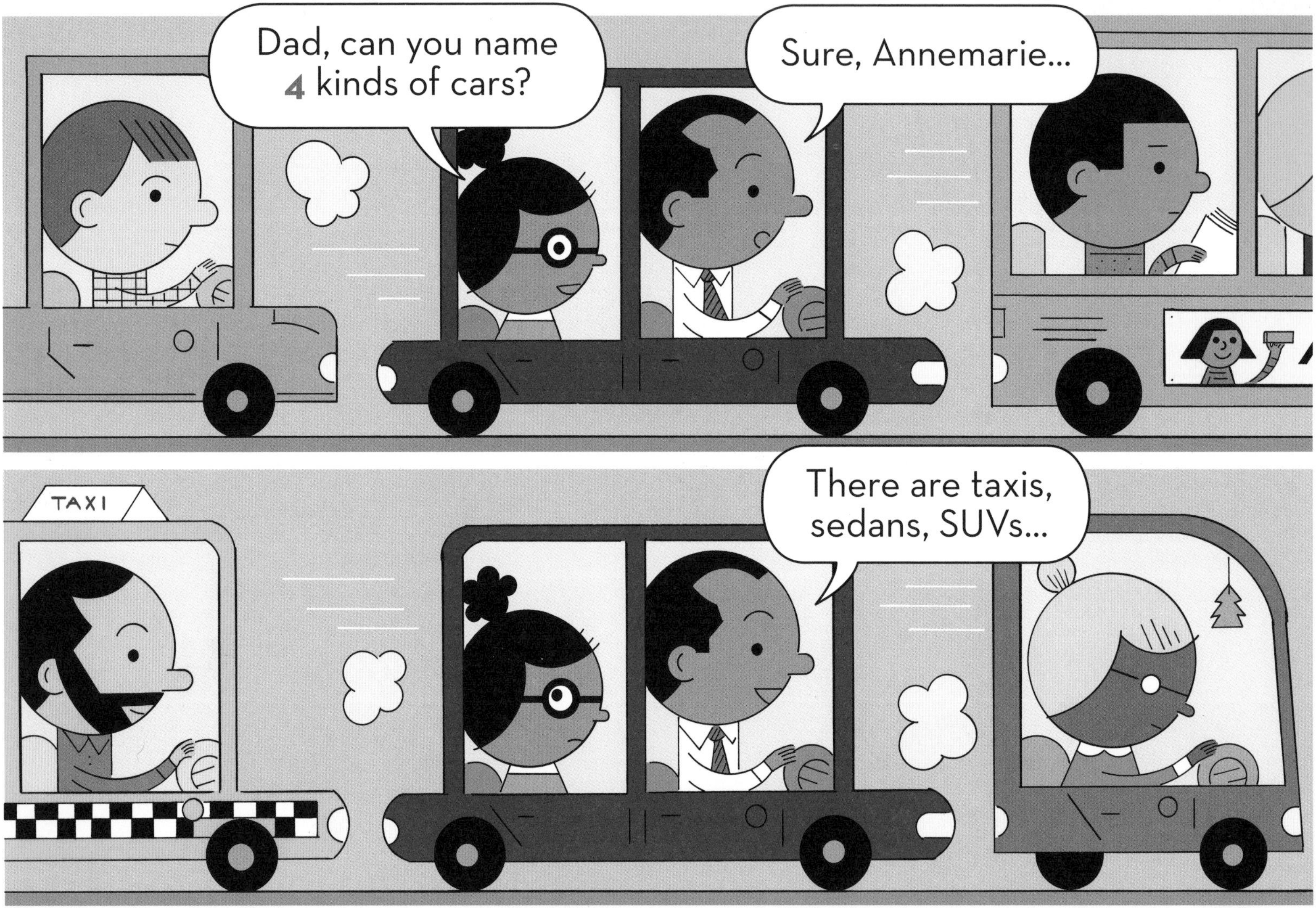
Dad, can you name 4 kinds of cars?
Sure, Annemarie...
TAXI
There are taxis, sedans, SUVs...

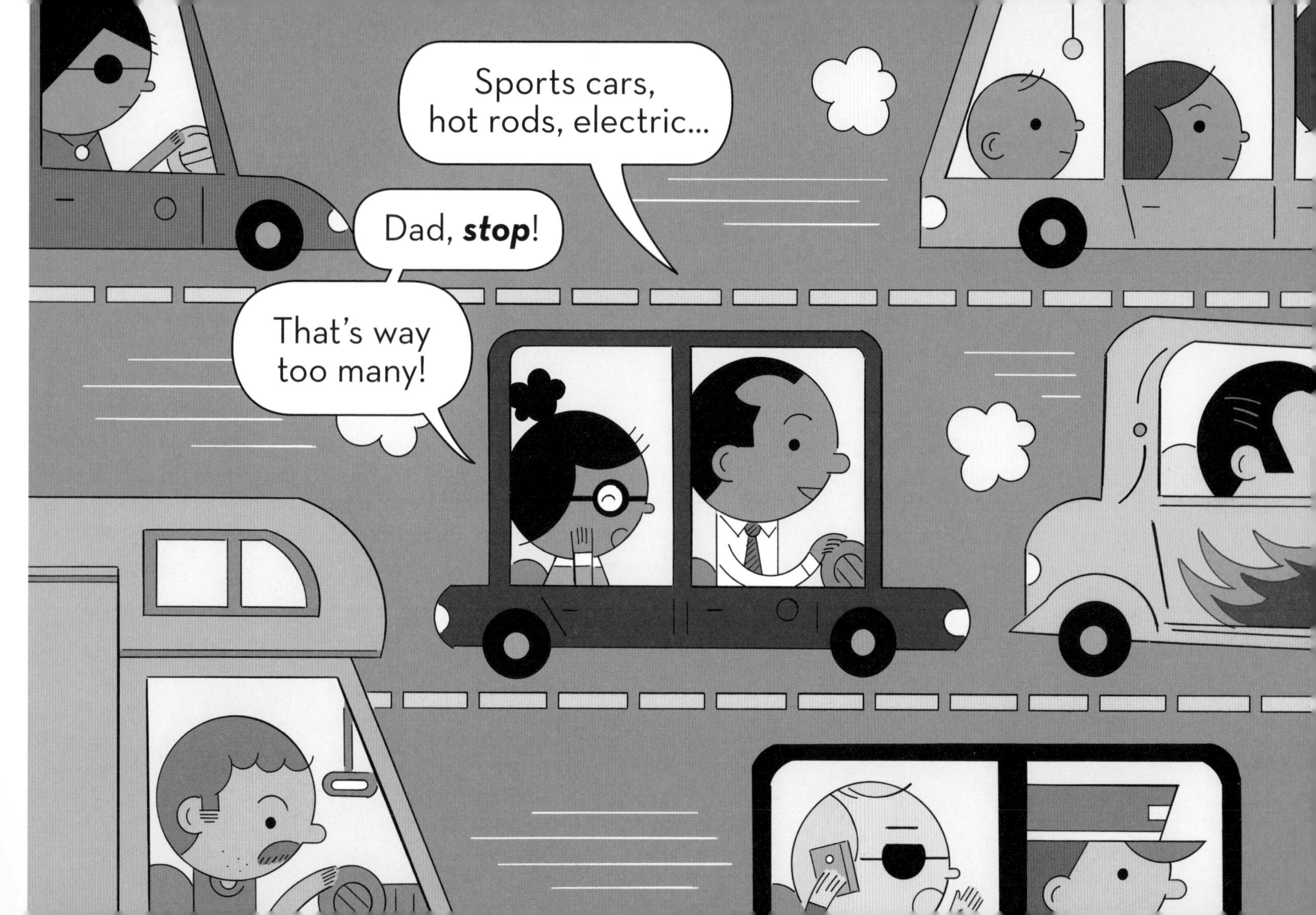
Sports cars, hot rods, electric...
Dad, **stop**!
That's way too many!

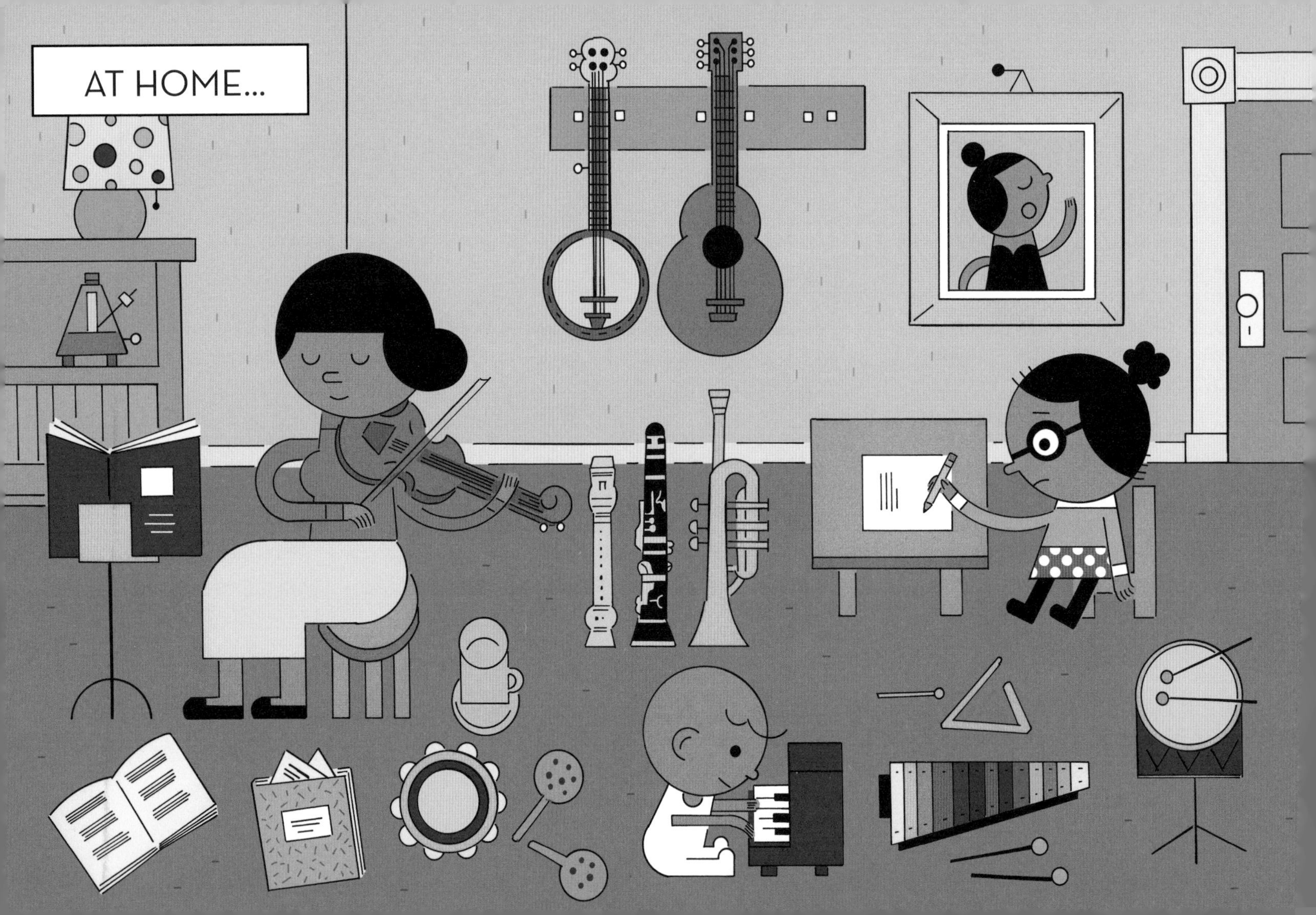
AT HOME...

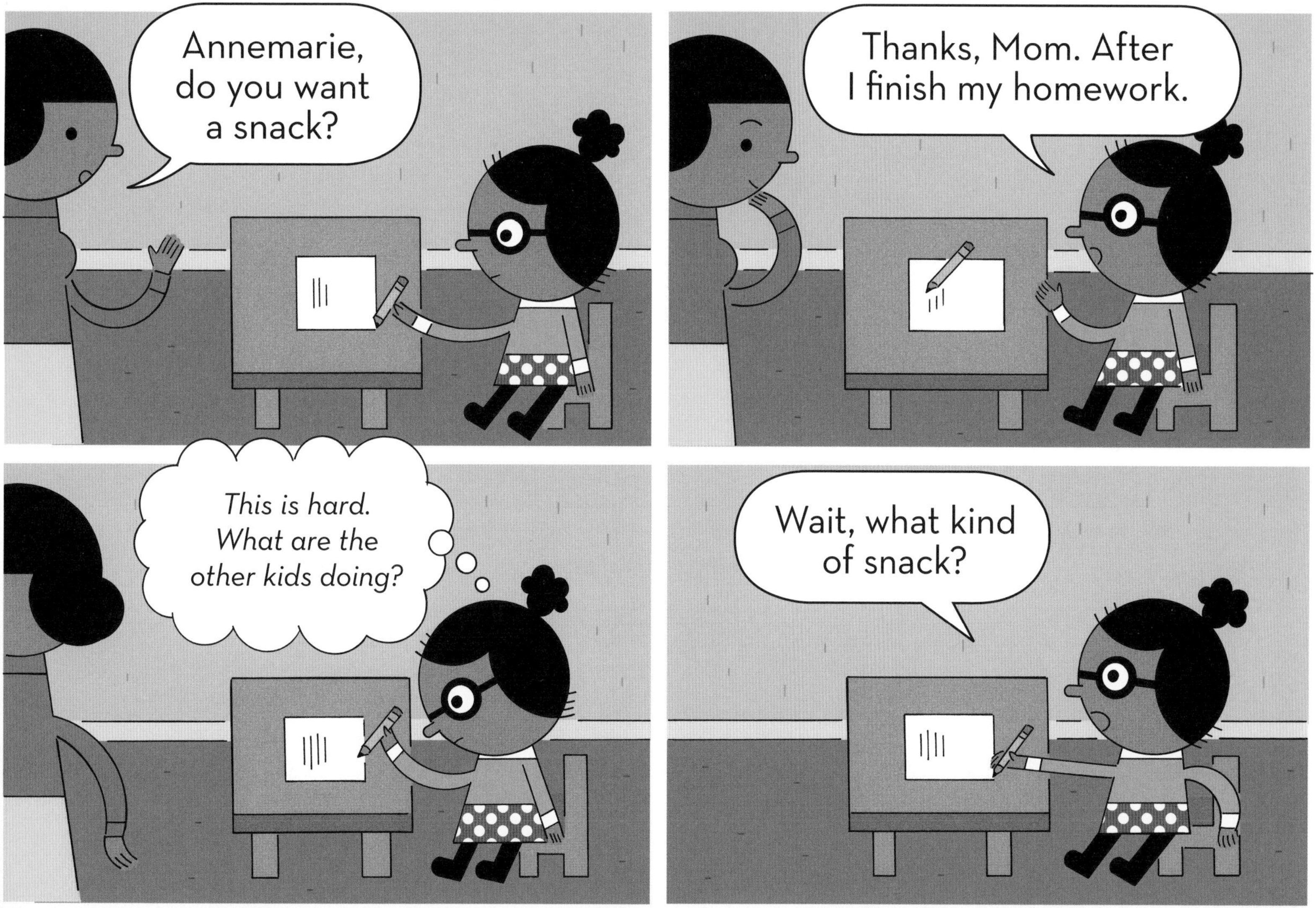
Annemarie, do you want a snack?
Thanks, Mom. After I finish my homework.
*This is hard. What are the other kids doing?*
Wait, what kind of snack?

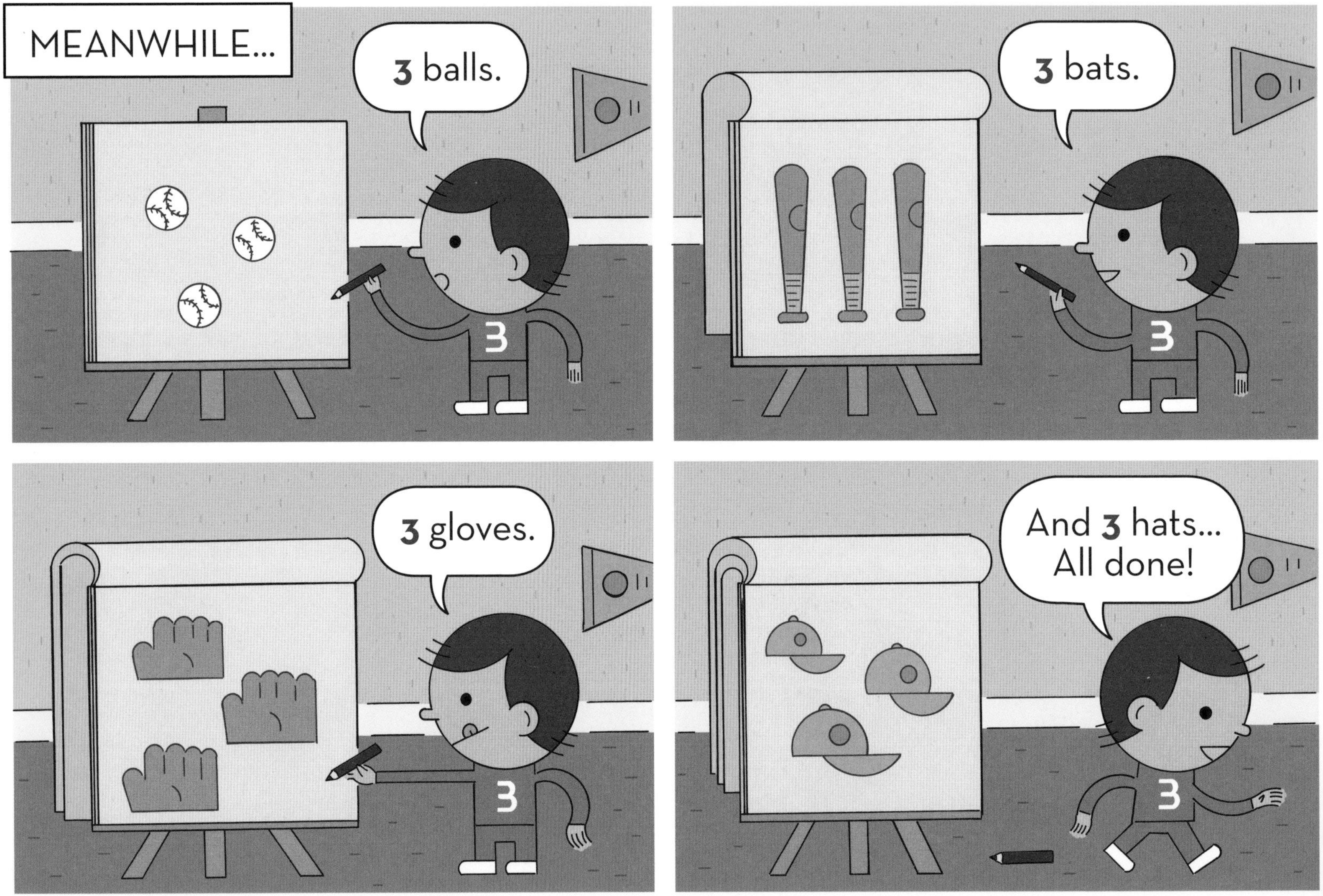
MEANWHILE...
3 balls.
3 bats.
3 gloves.
And 3 hats...
All done!

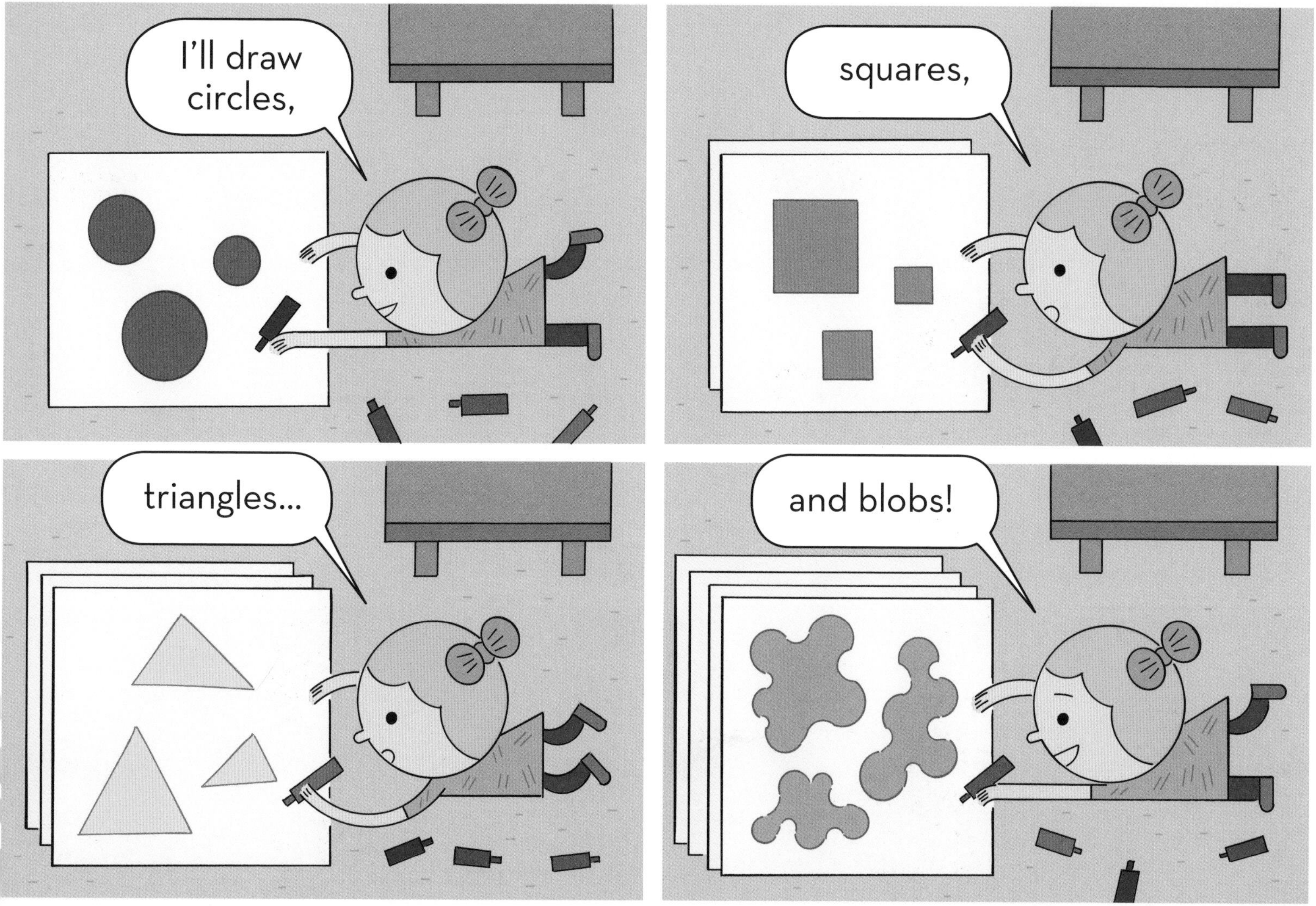
I'll draw circles,
squares,
triangles...
and blobs!

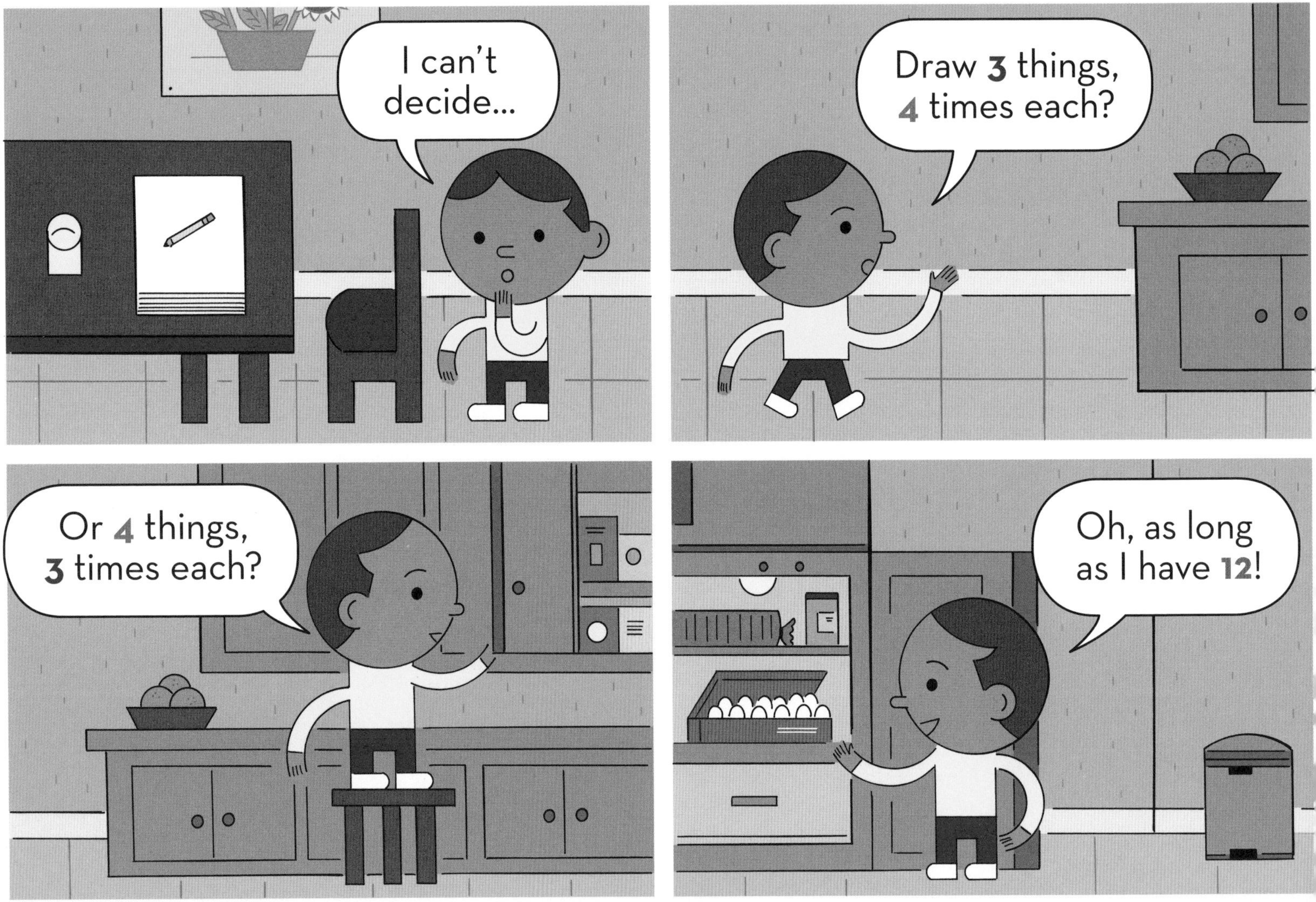
I can't decide...
Draw 3 things, 4 times each?
Or 4 things, 3 times each?
Oh, as long as I have 12!

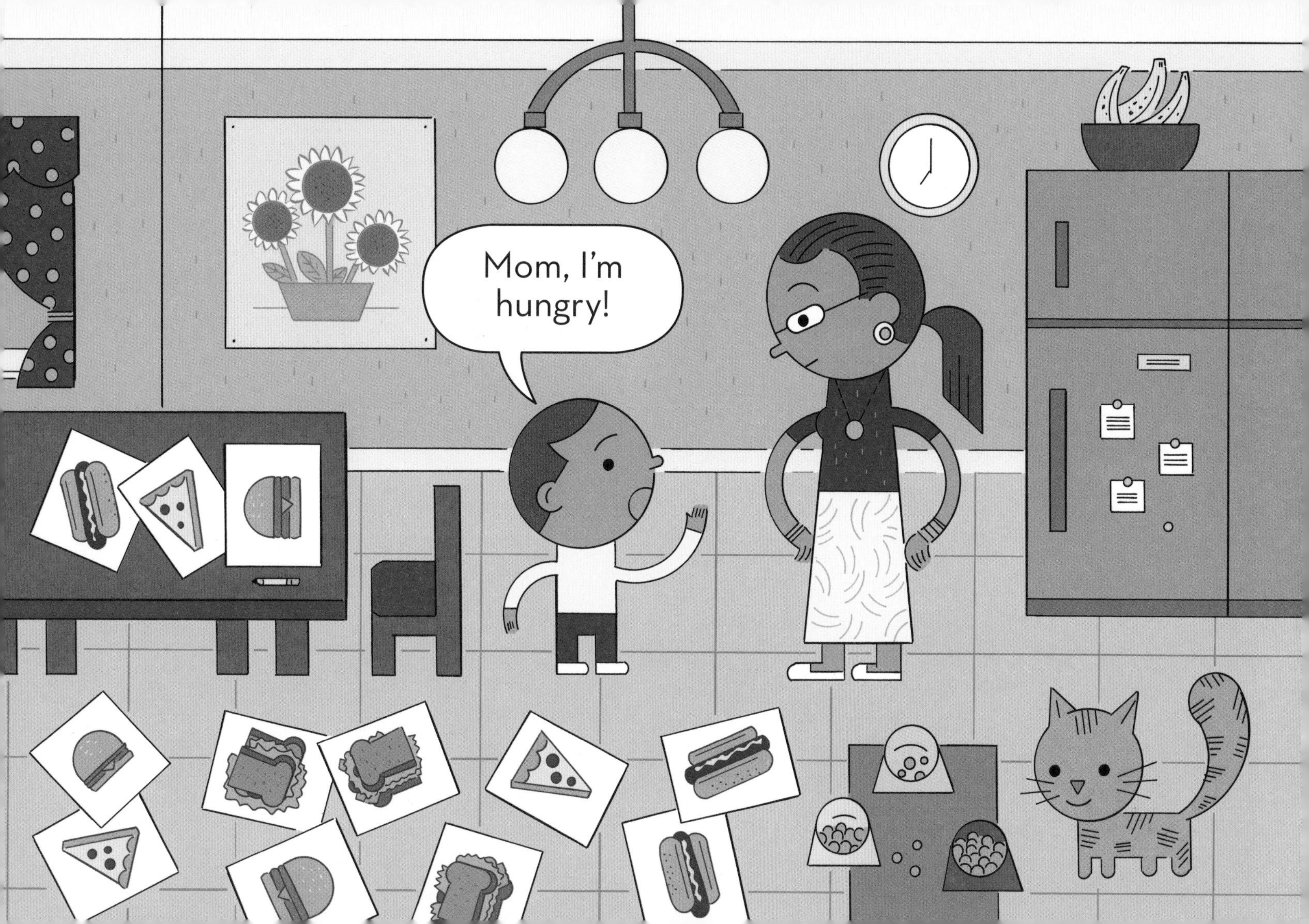
Mom, I'm hungry!

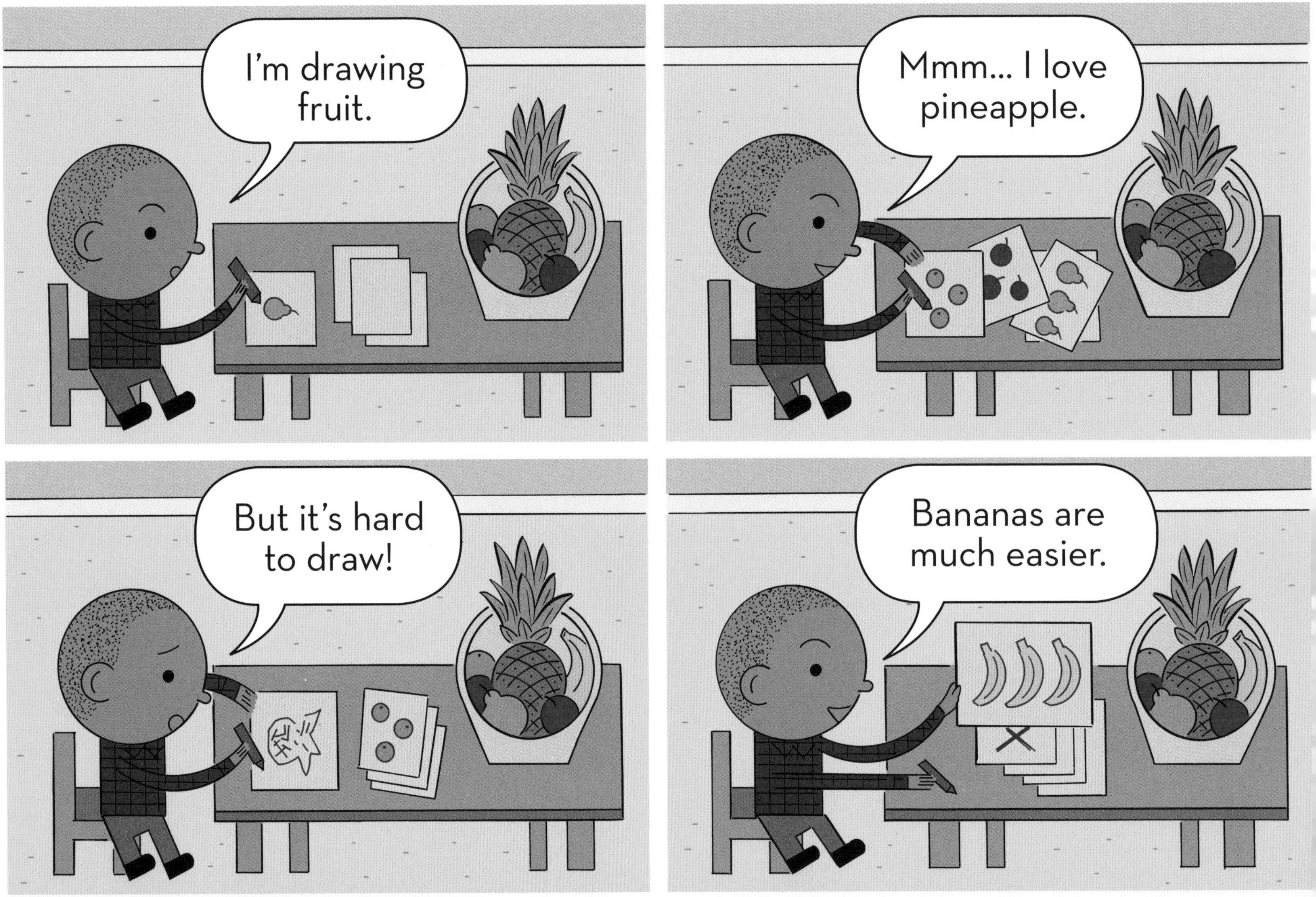
I'm drawing fruit.
Mmm... I love pineapple.
But it's hard to draw!
Bananas are much easier.

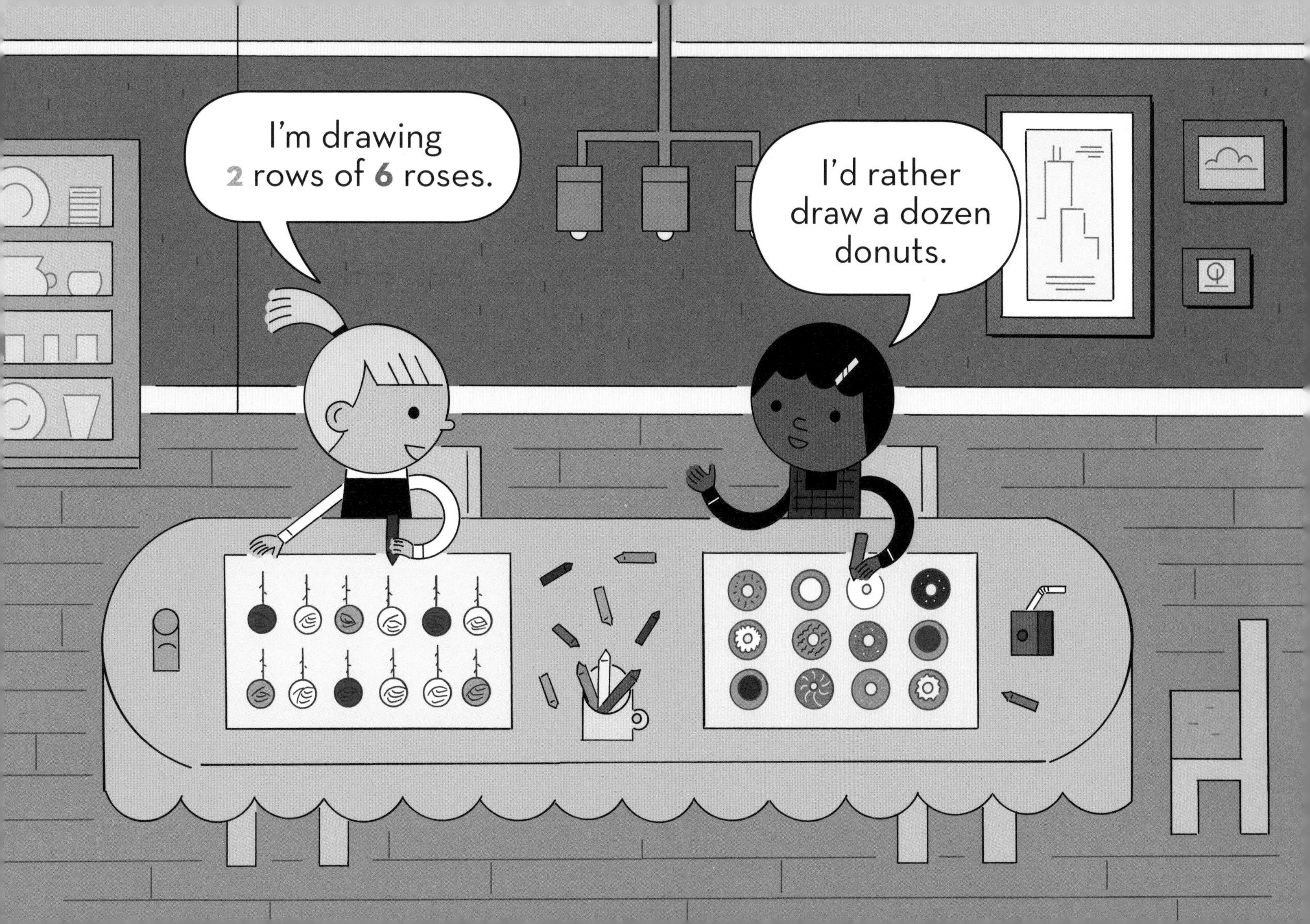
I'm drawing 2 rows of 6 roses.
I'd rather draw a dozen donuts.

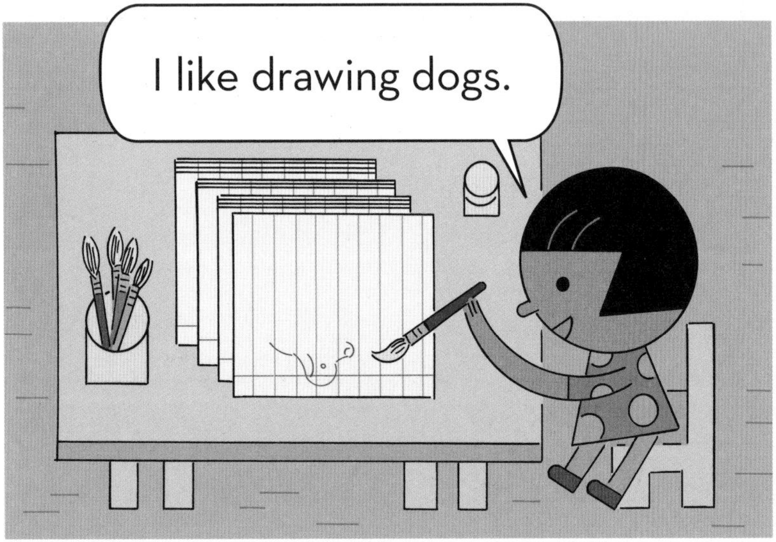
I like drawing dogs.

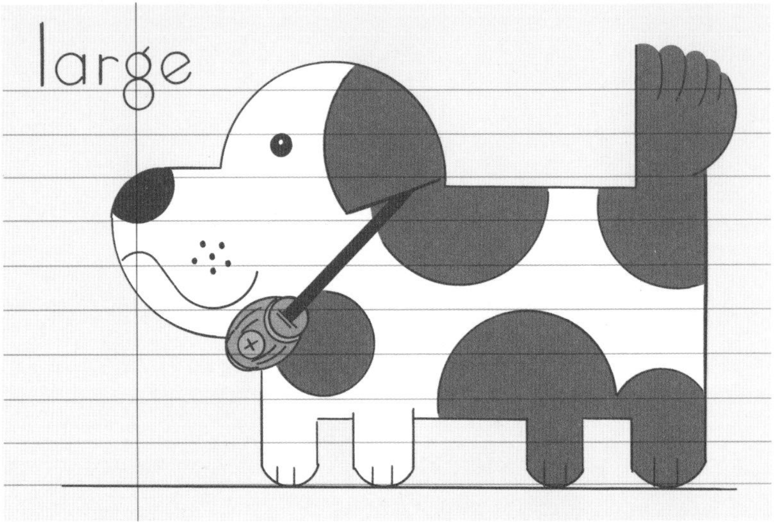
large

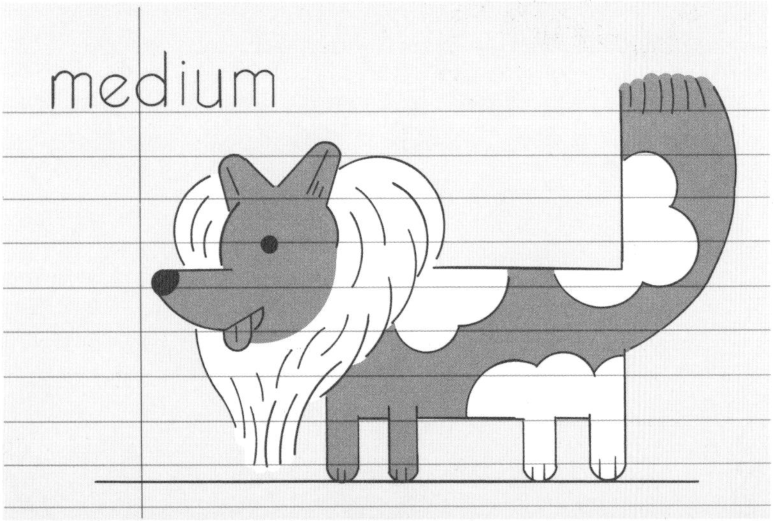
medium

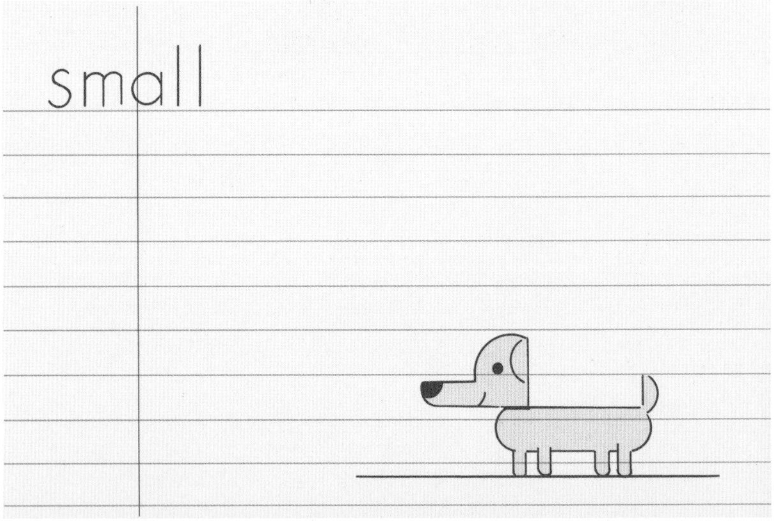
small

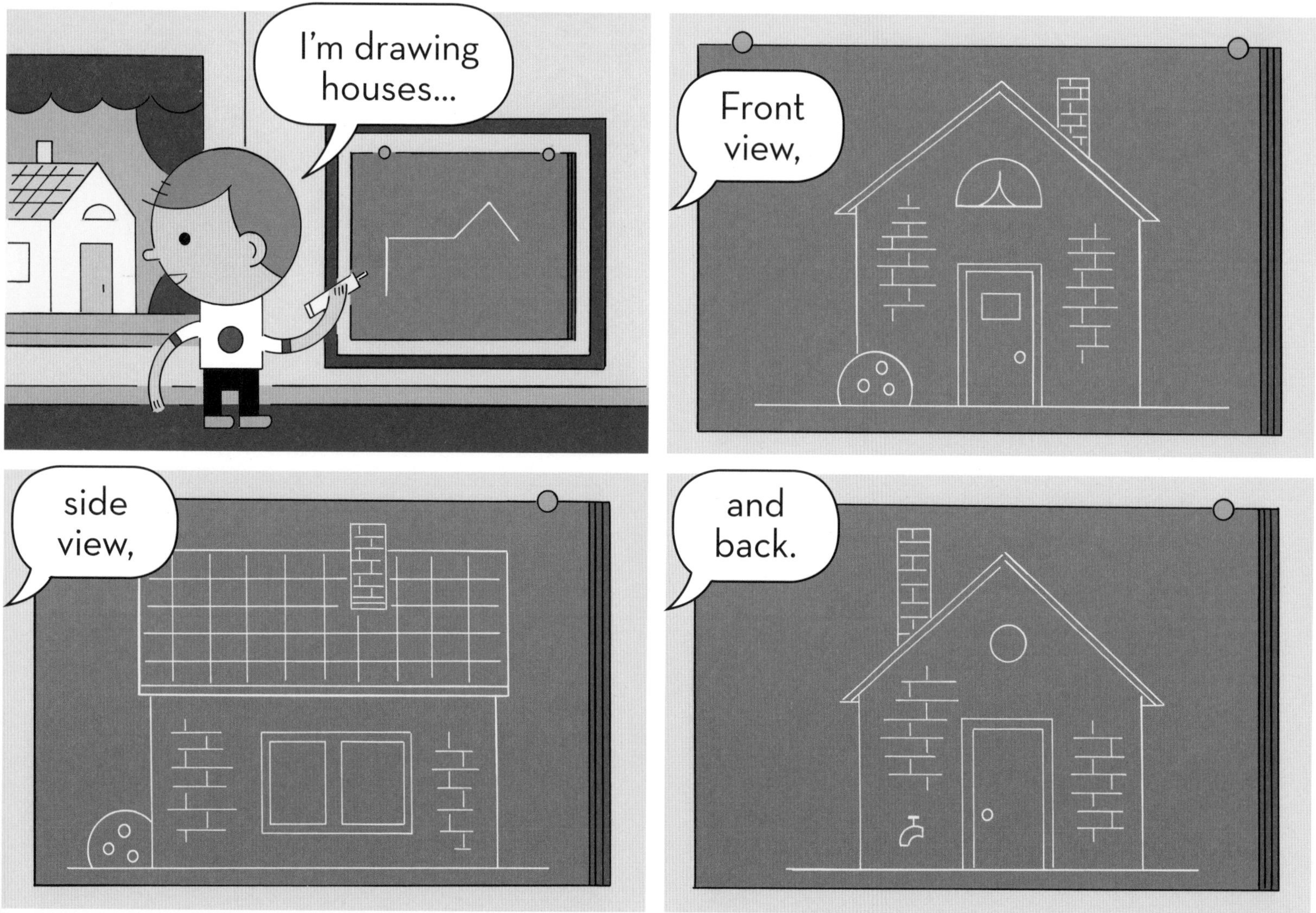
I'm drawing houses...
Front view,
side view,
and back.

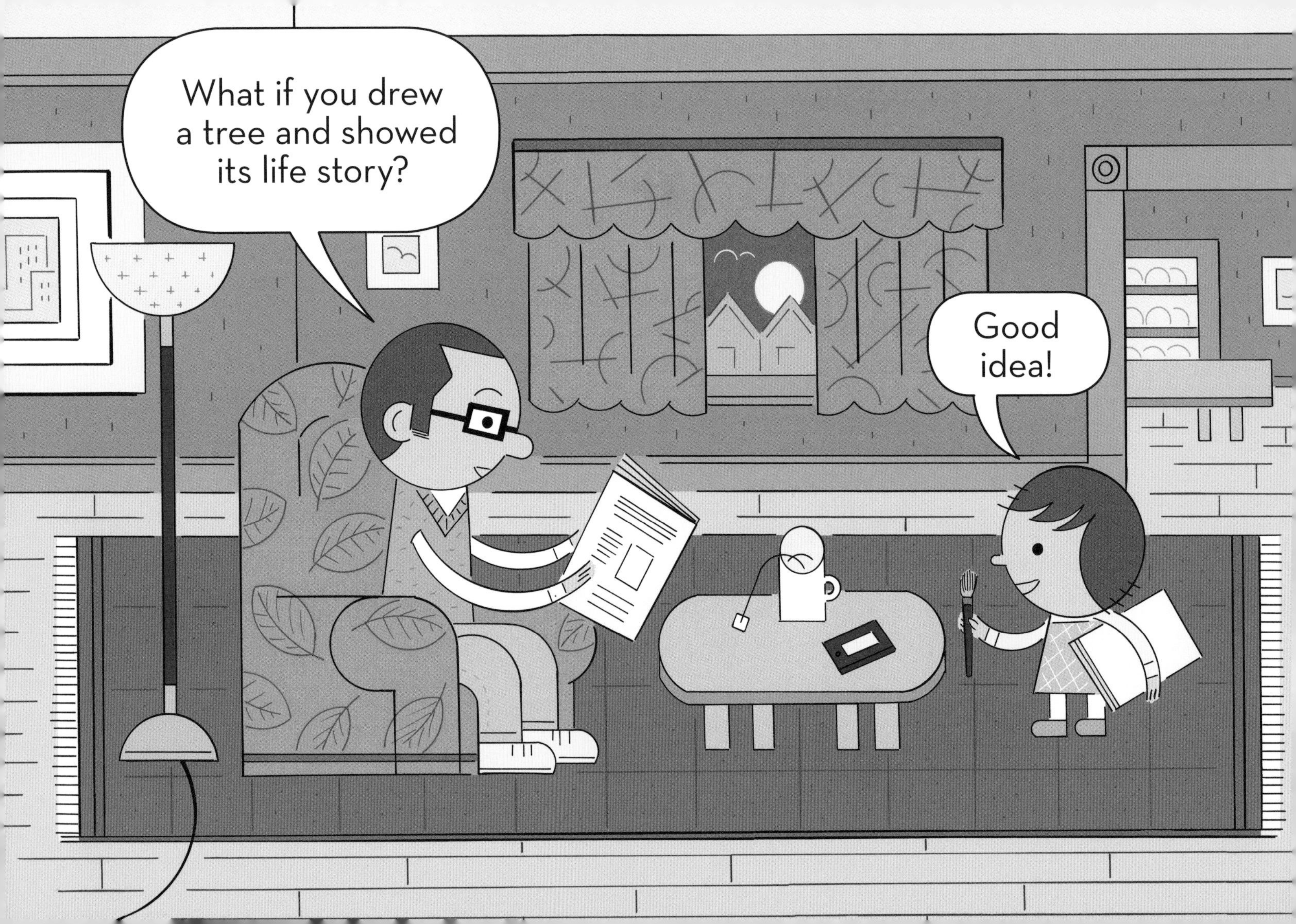
What if you drew a tree and showed its life story?
Good idea!

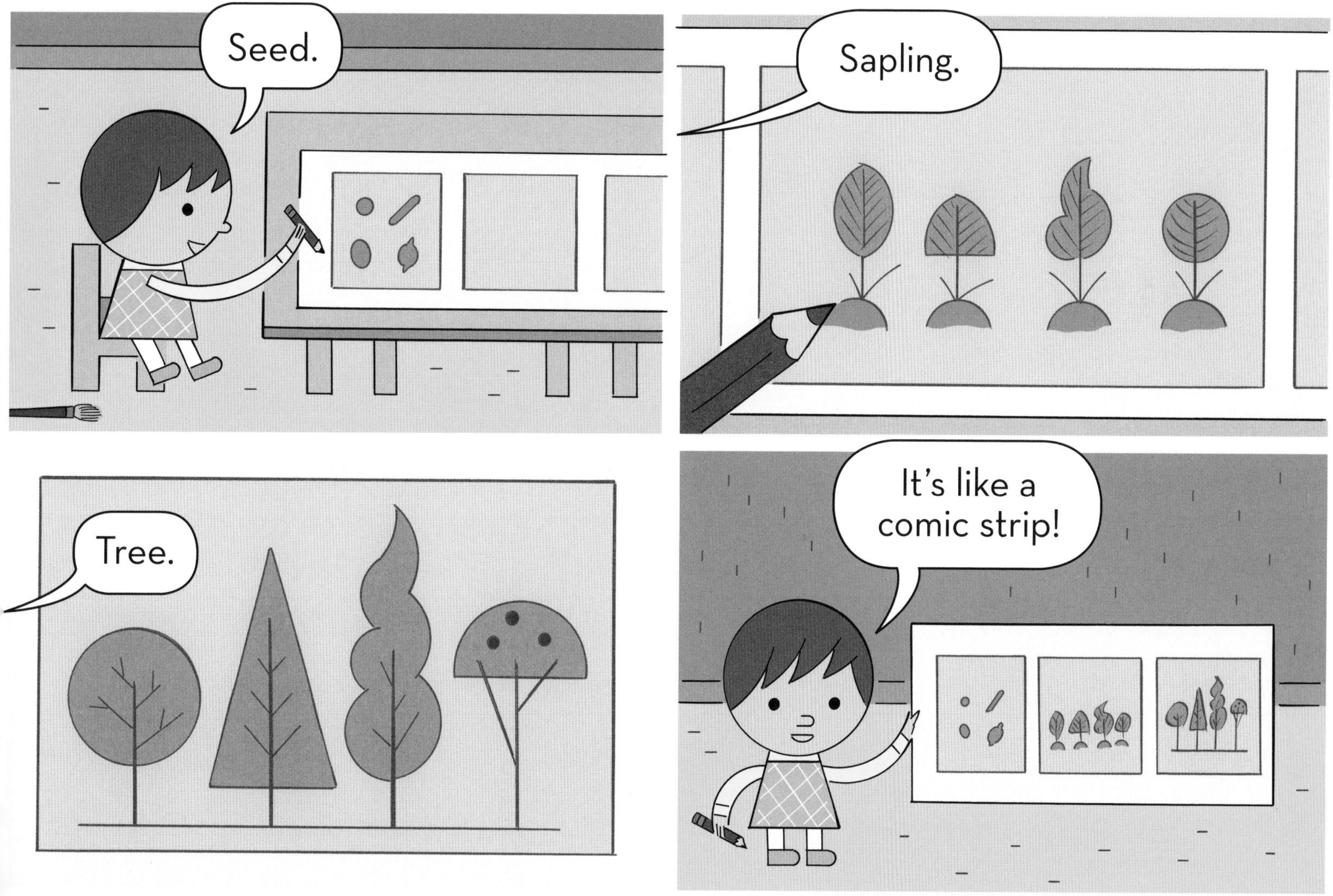
Seed.
Sapling.
Tree.
It's like a comic strip!

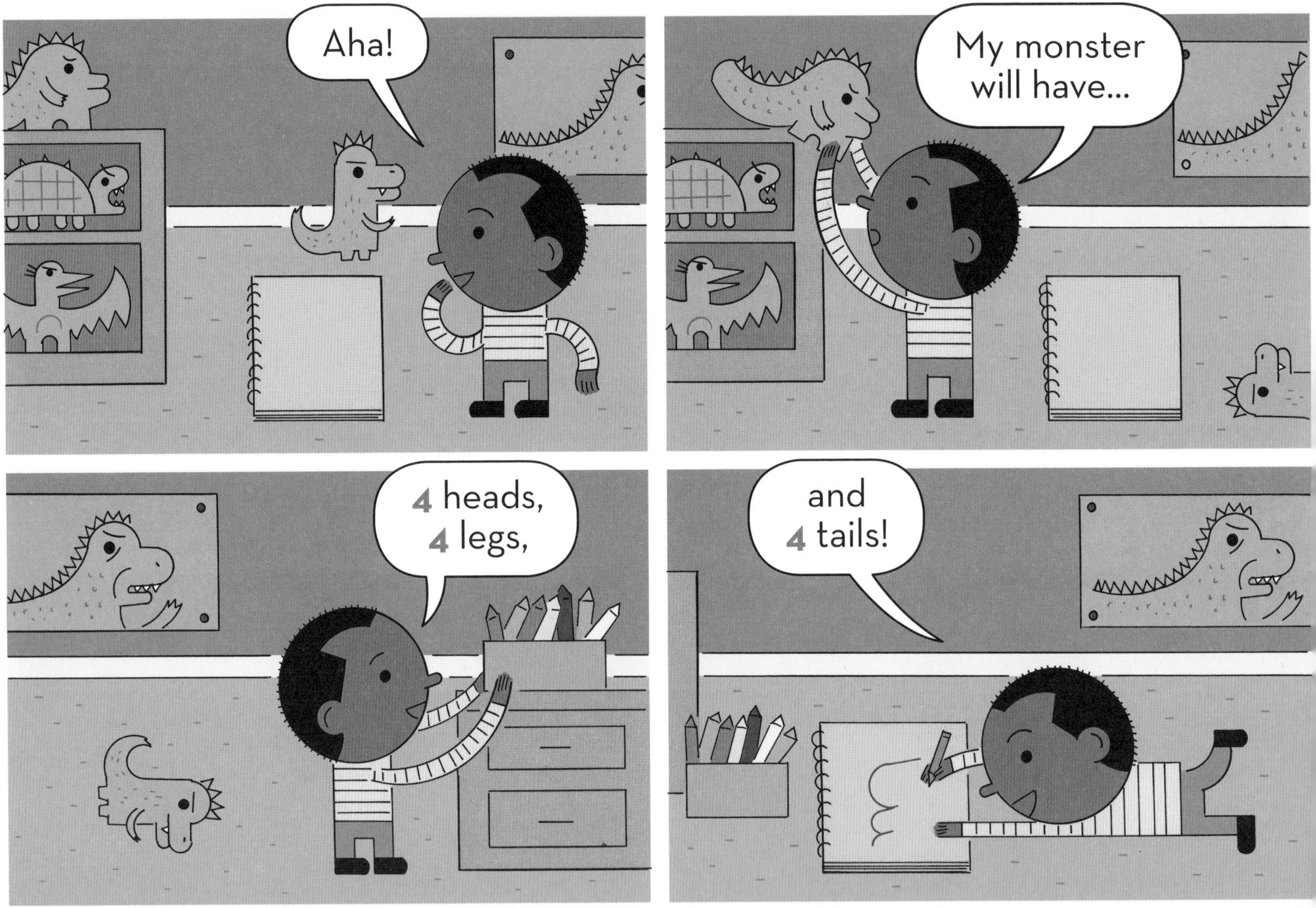

Aha!
My monster will have...
4 heads, 4 legs,
and 4 tails!

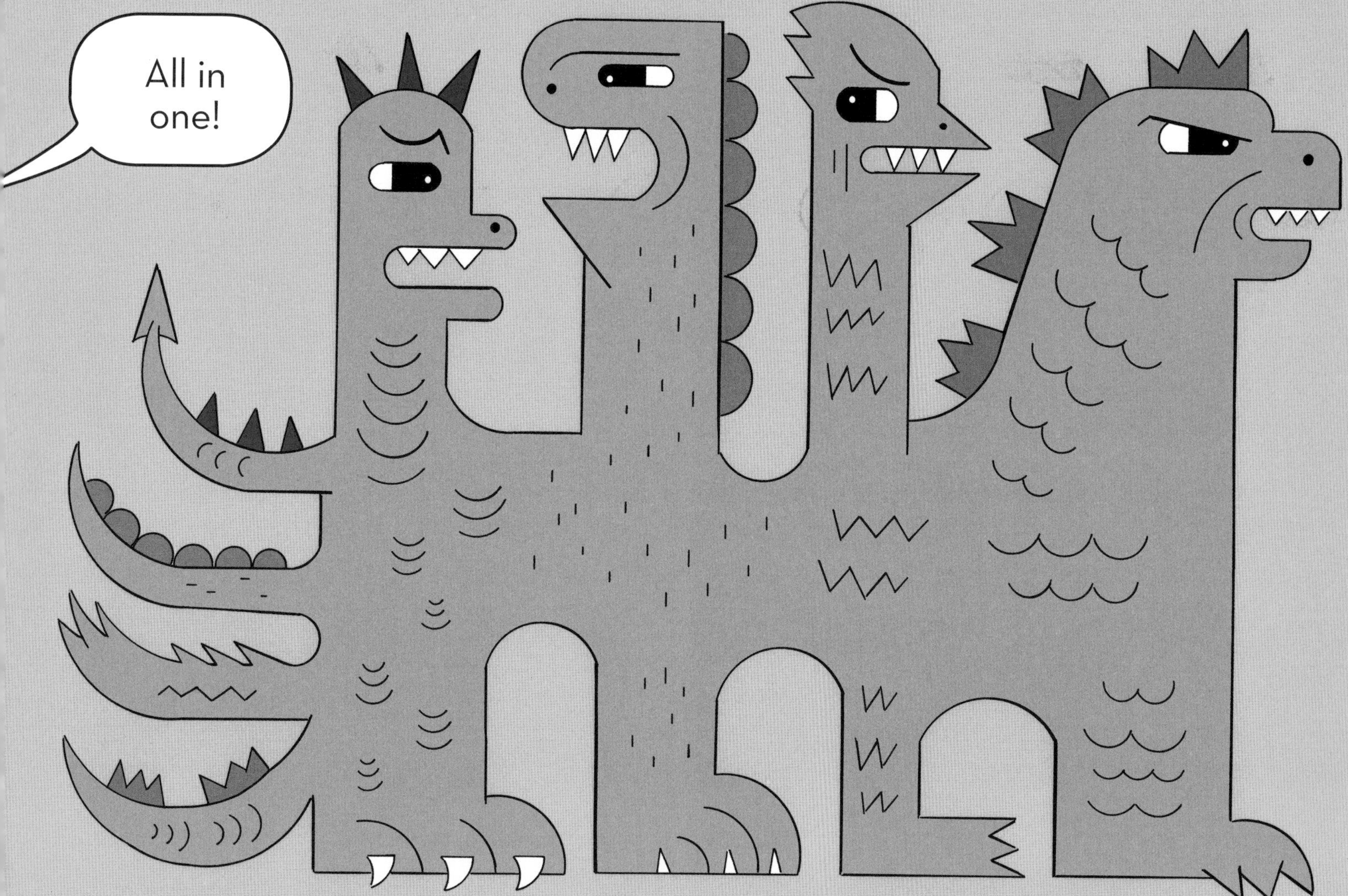
All in one!

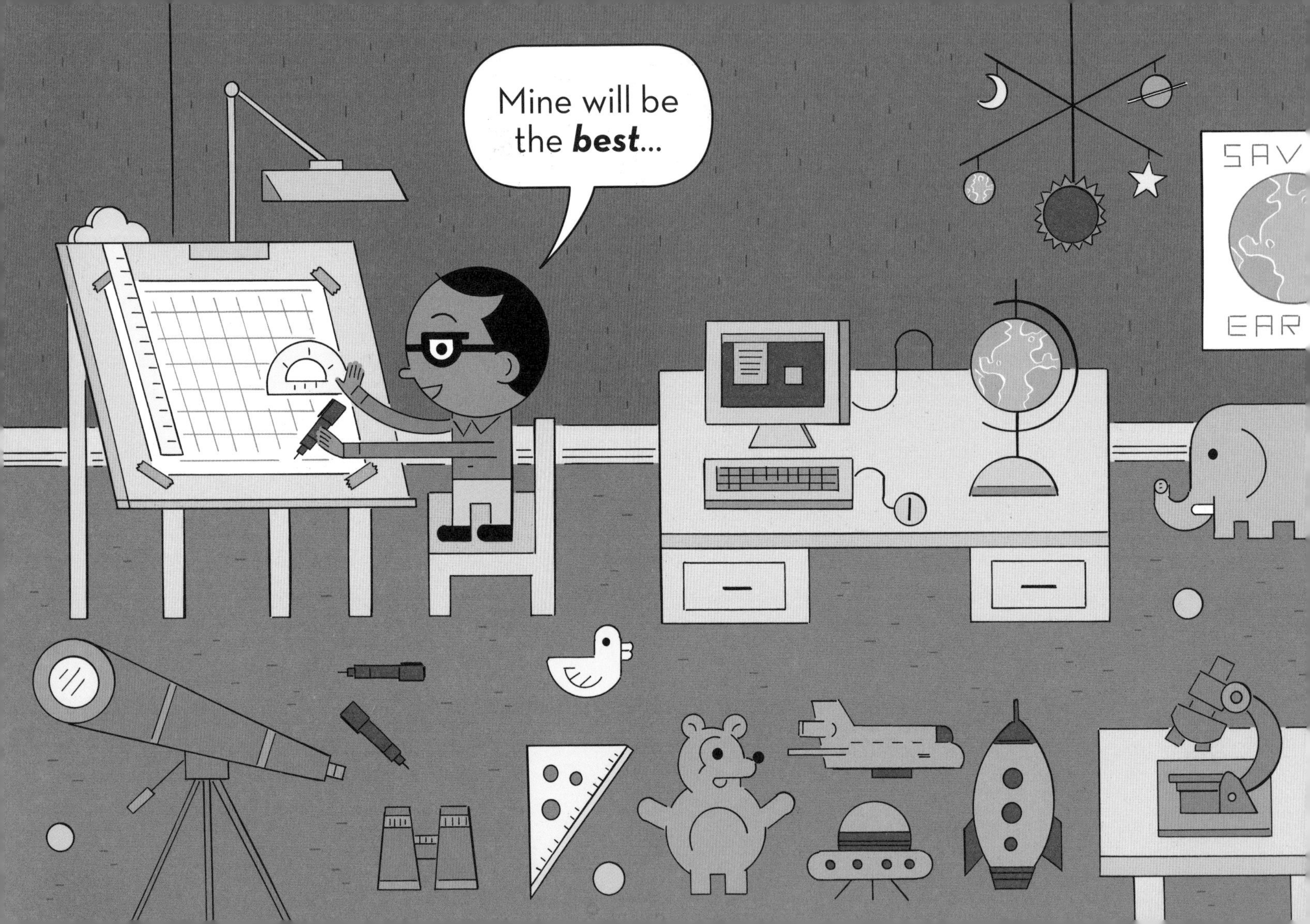
Mine will be the ***best***...

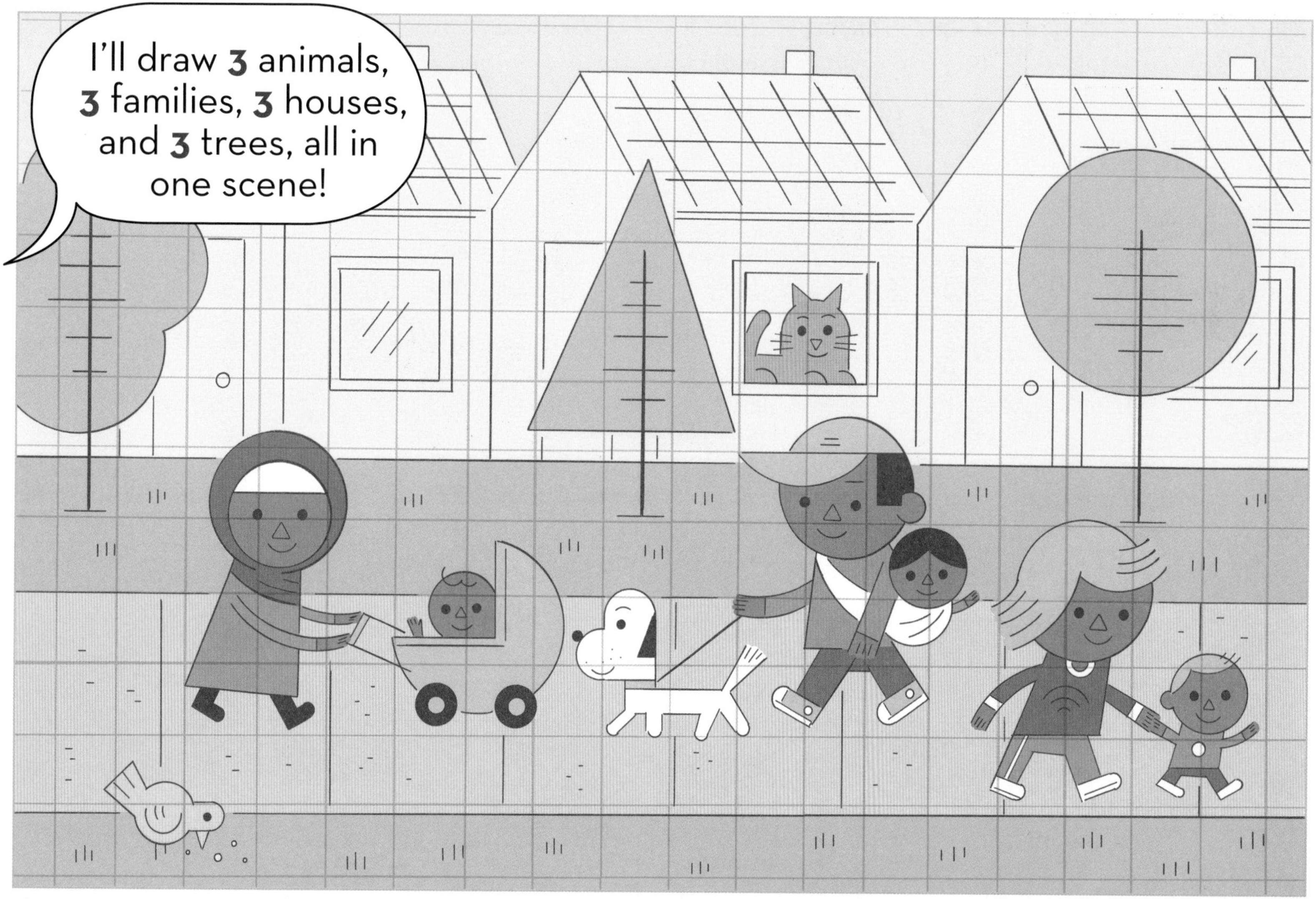
I'll draw **3** animals, **3** families, **3** houses, and **3** trees, all in one scene!

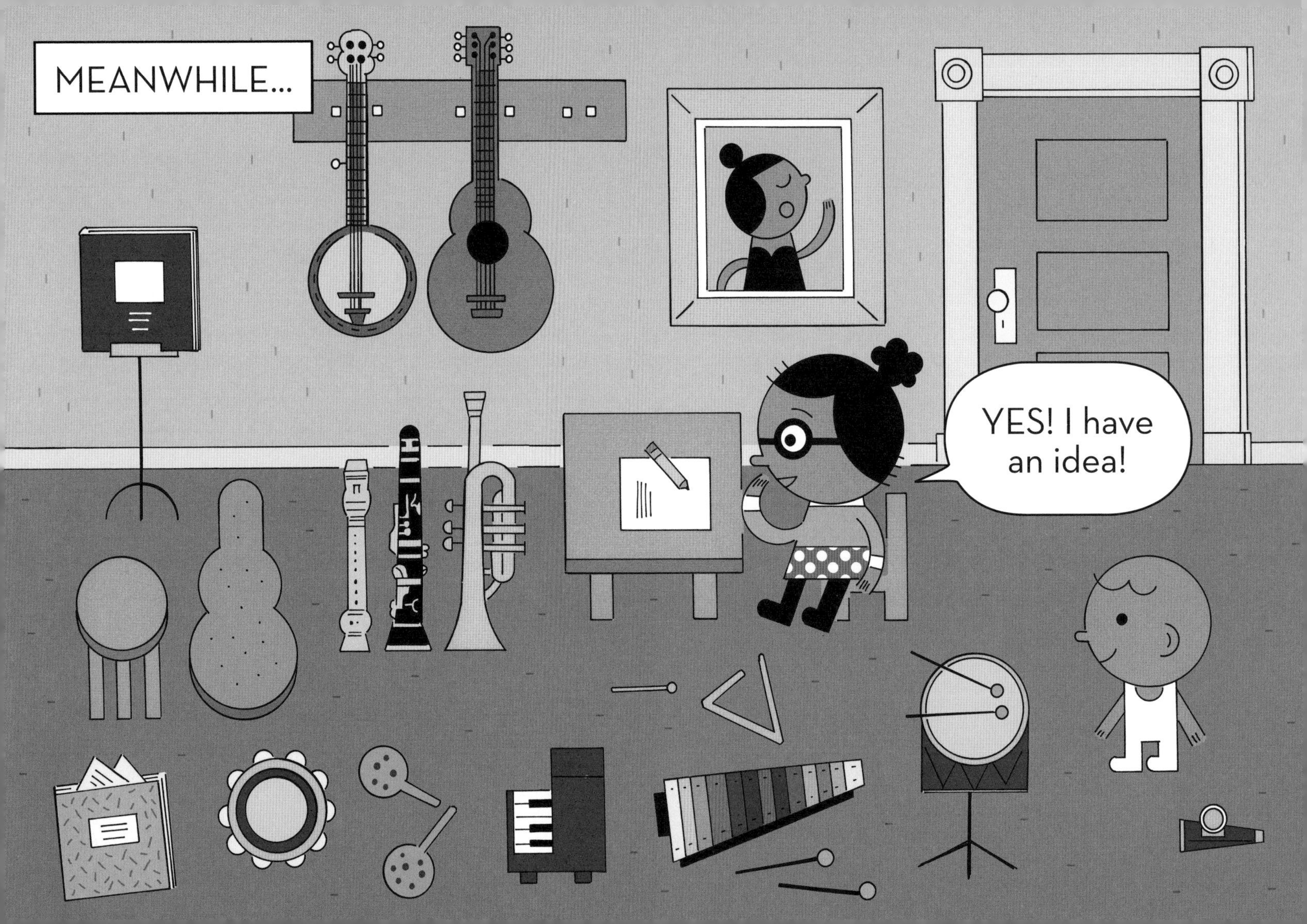
MEANWHILE...
YES! I have an idea!

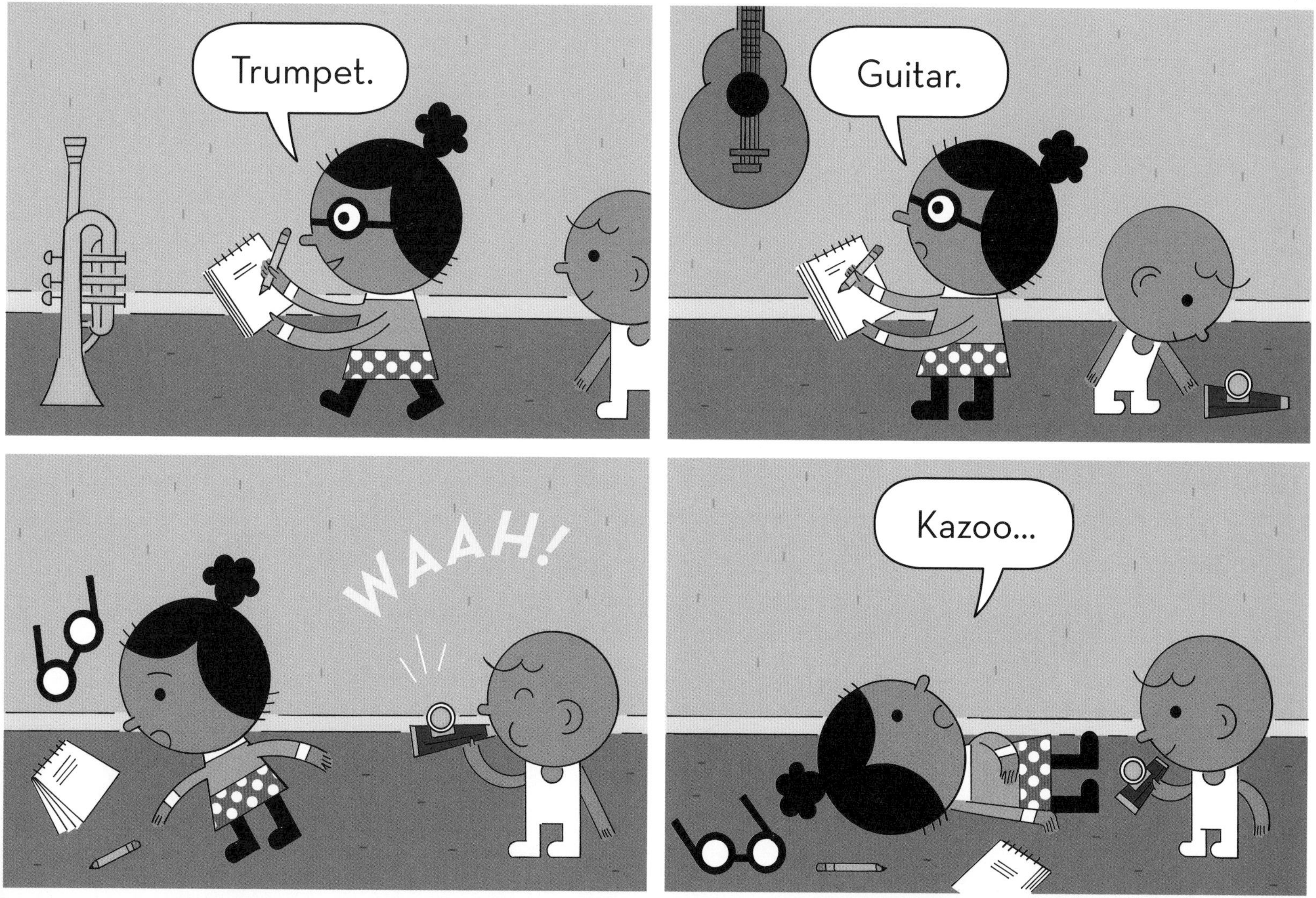
Trumpet.
Guitar.
WAAH!
Kazoo...

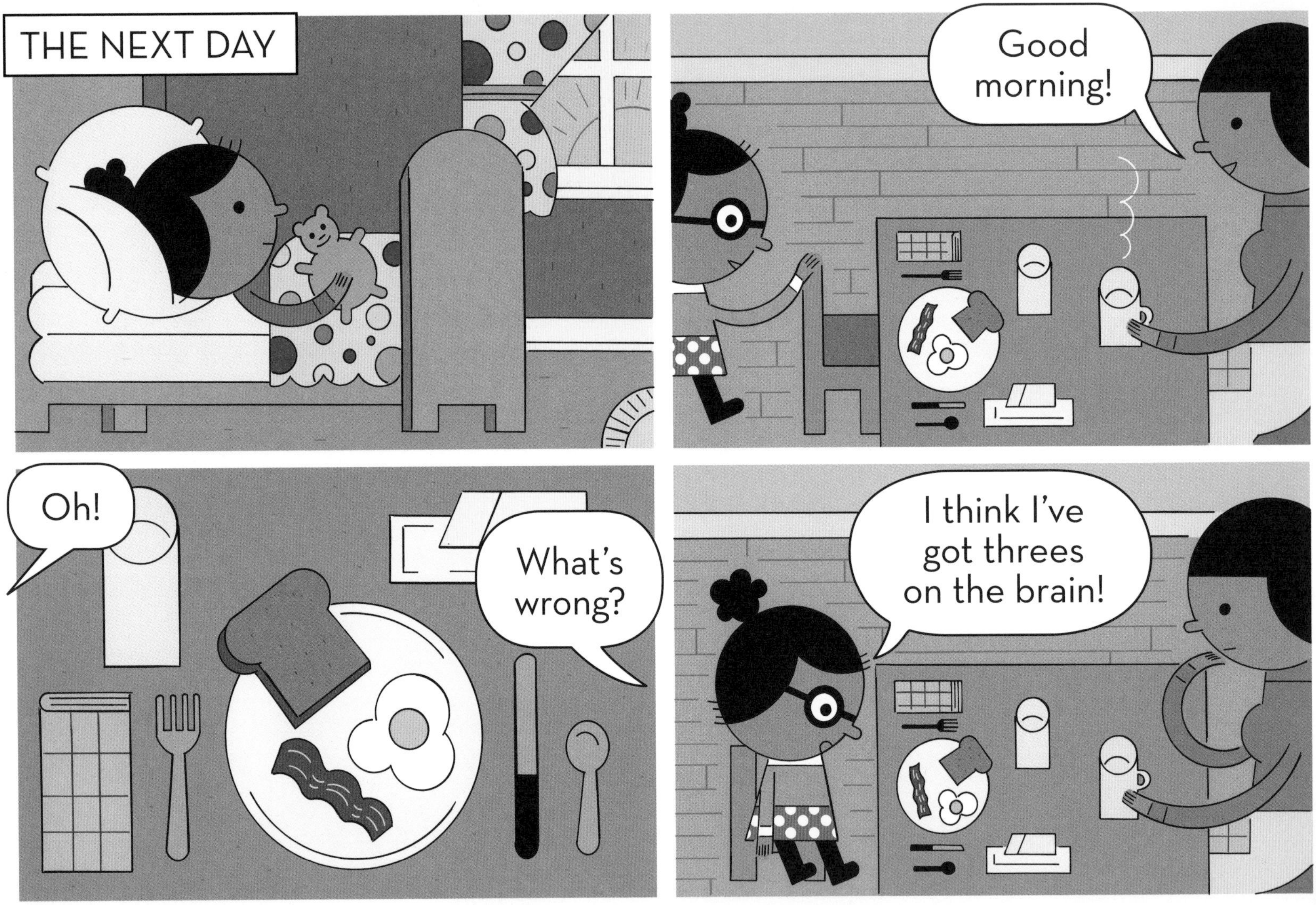
THE NEXT DAY
Good morning!
Oh!
What's wrong?
I think I've got threes on the brain!

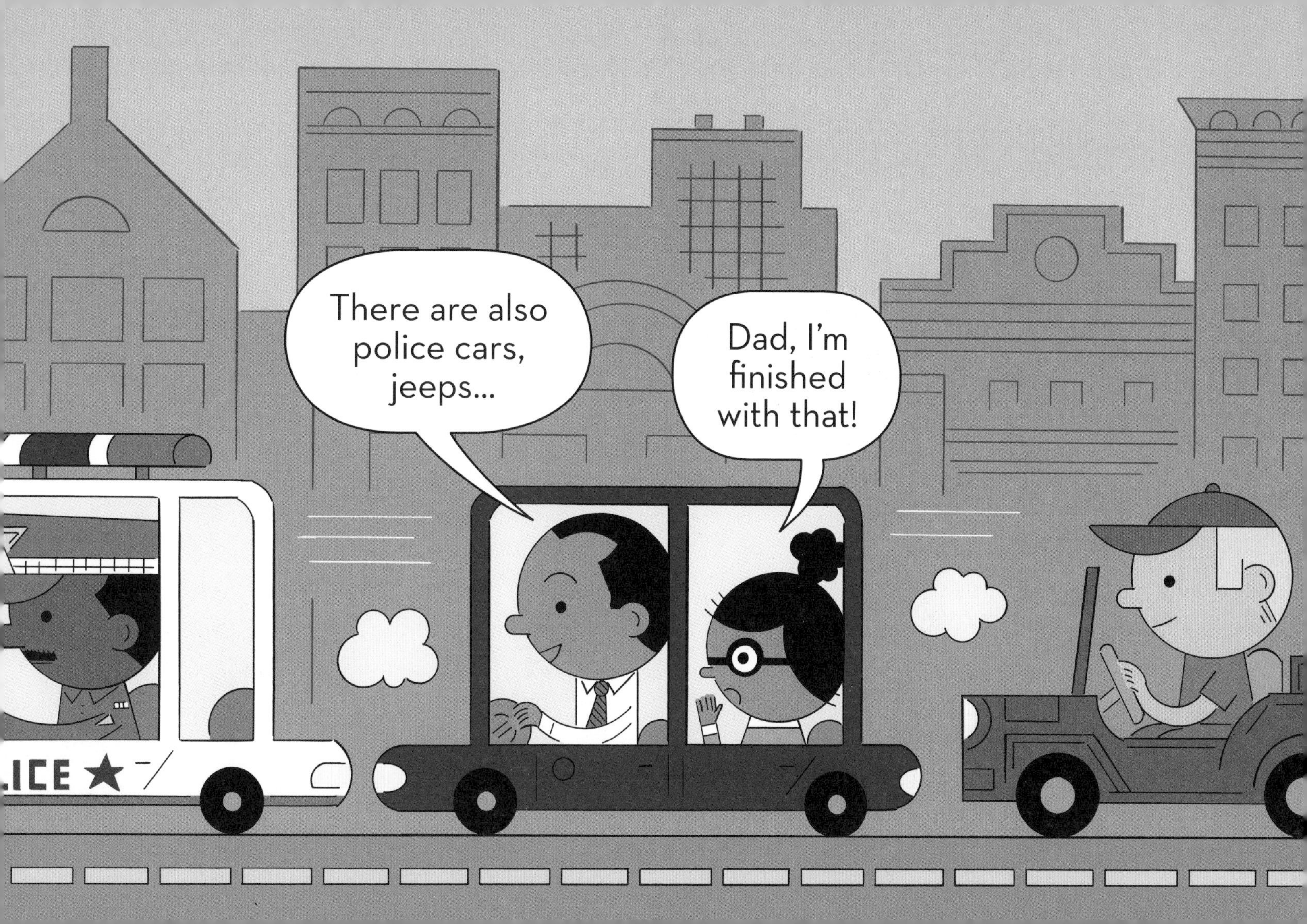
There are also police cars, jeeps...
Dad, I'm finished with that!
LICE

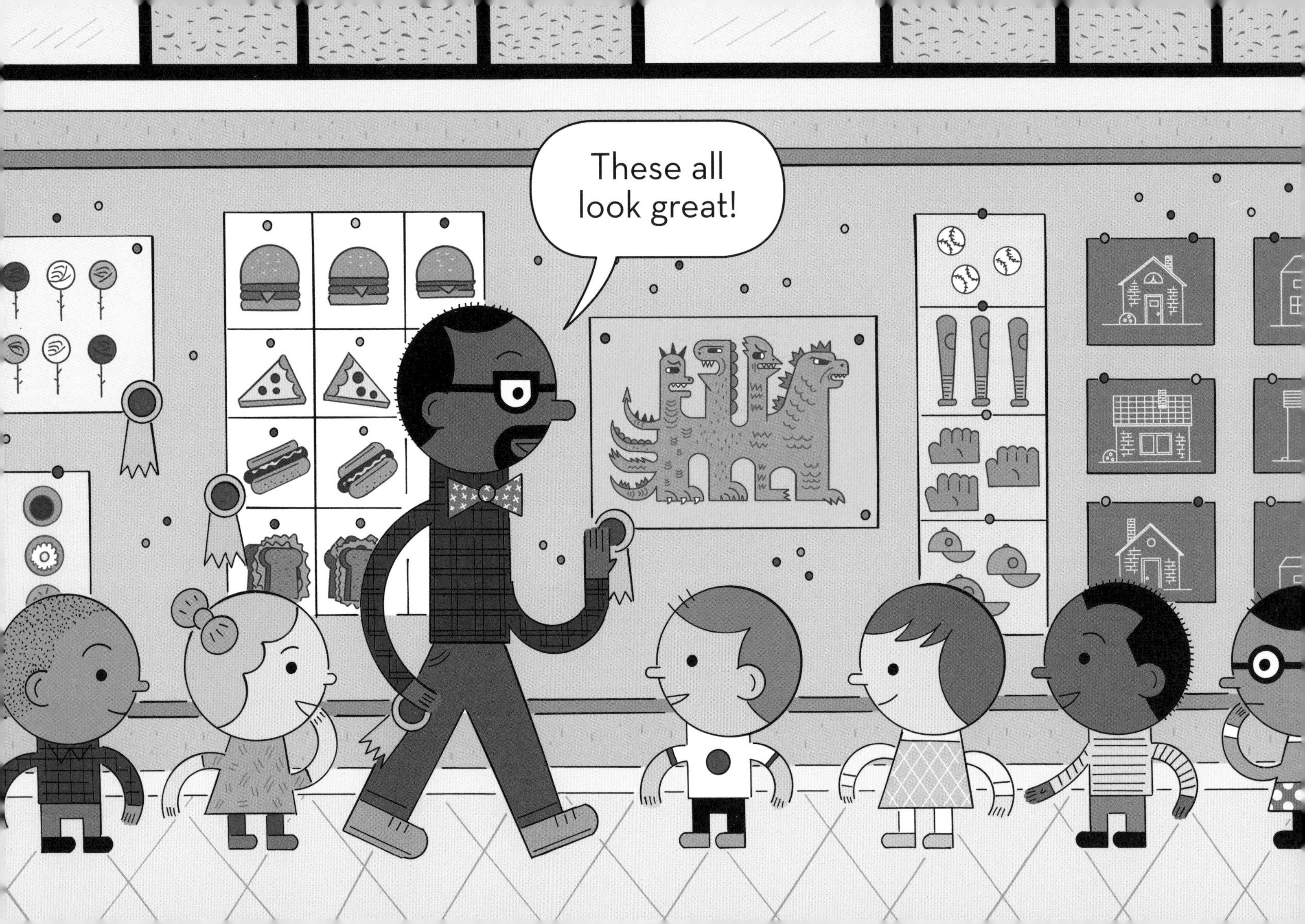
These all look great!

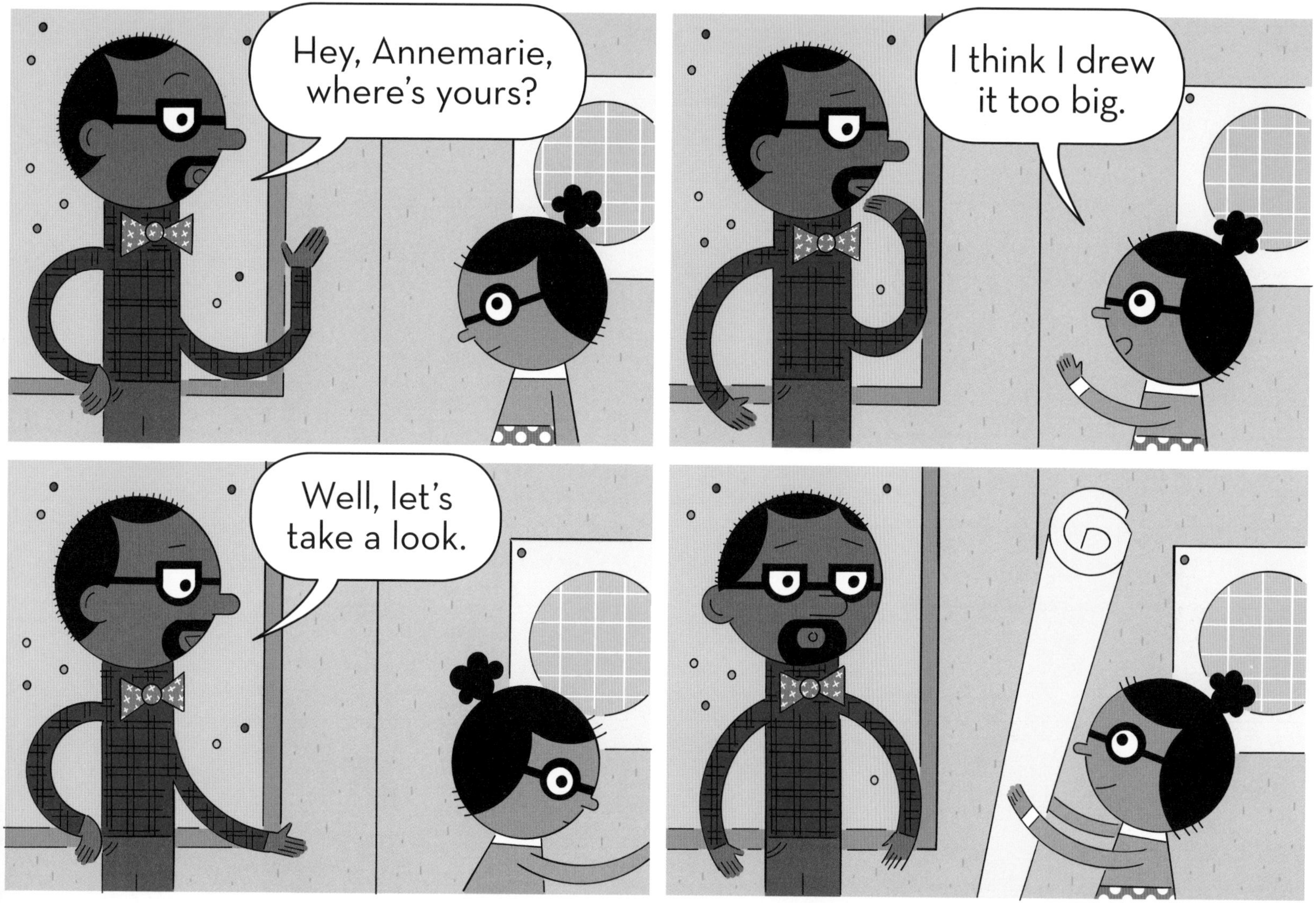
Hey, Annemarie, where's yours?
I think I drew it too big.
Well, let's take a look.

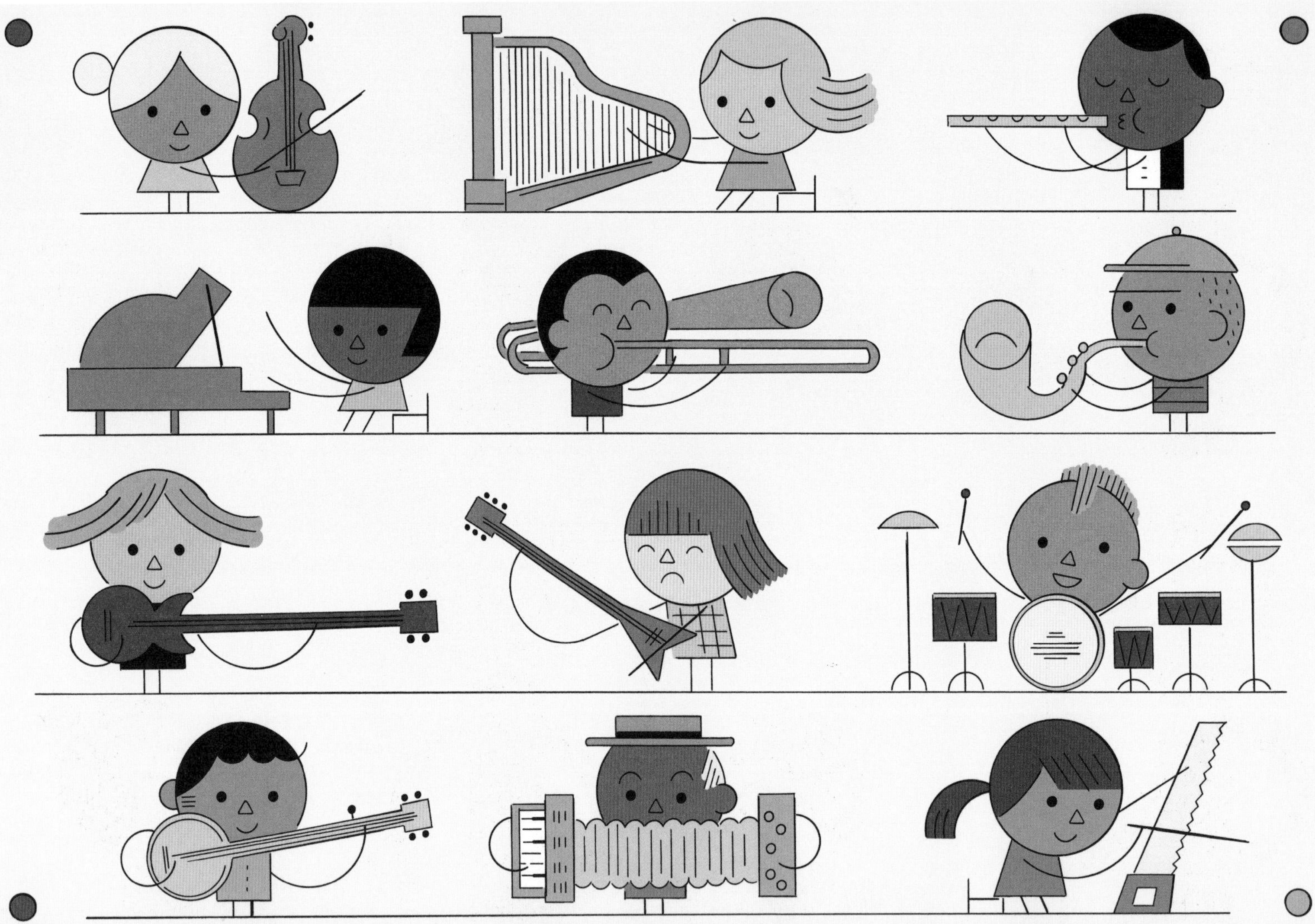

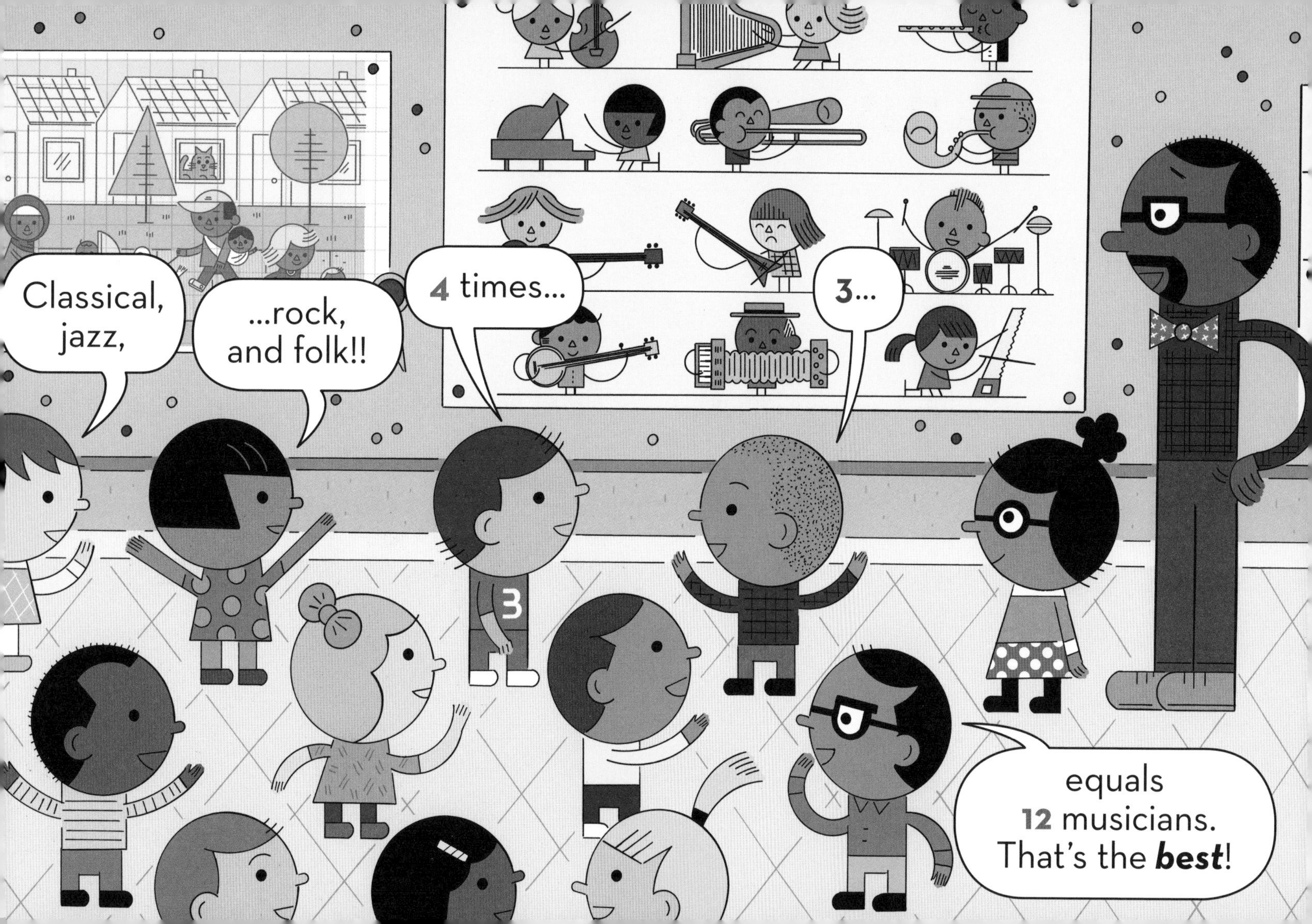
Classical, jazz,
...rock, and folk!!
4 times...
3...
equals 12 musicians. That's the *best*!

# ABOUT THE AUTHOR

**IVAN BRUNETTI** is an art teacher as well as an artist and a cartoonist. He has assigned drawing sets of 3 to his own students – but since they are college-aged, they have the extra challenge of making 25 sets of 3 things each. Ivan has published many acclaimed books for adults, including *Cartooning: Philosophy and Practice*. *Wordplay*, about compound words, was his first book for children. From a young age, Ivan loved playing with words and numbers. He also likes to play with his readers: look for all the 3s hidden throughout the book. Even today, Ivan still has to count to fall asleep. "Seeing the world as groups of numbers helps me make sense of things. And it never gets old because math has so many mysteries."

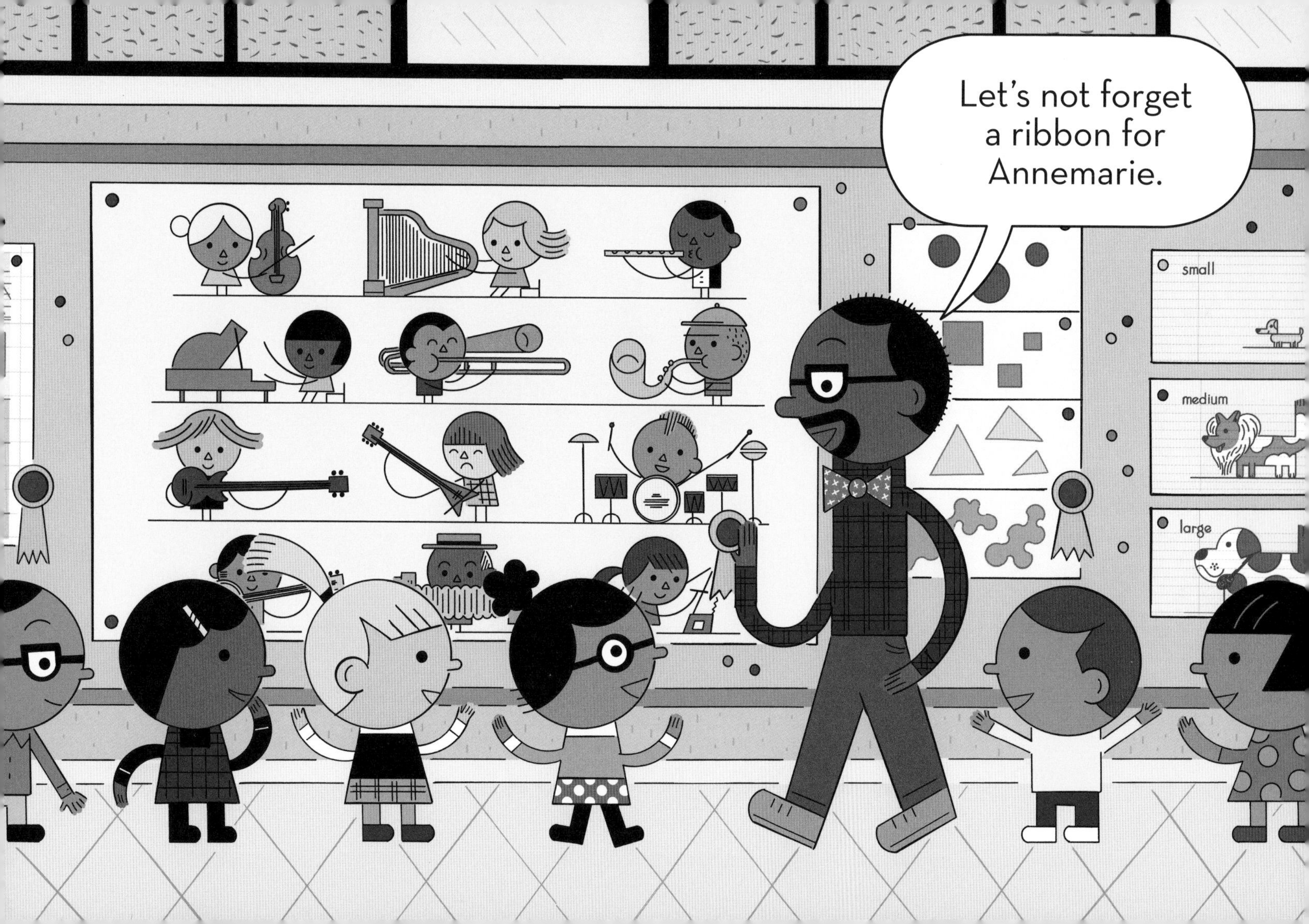
Let's not forget a ribbon for Annemarie.
small
medium
large

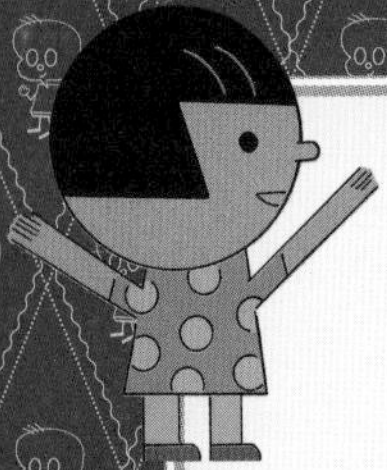

TIPS FOR PARENTS AND TEACHERS:

# HOW TO READ COMICS WITH KIDS

Kids love comics! They are naturally drawn to the details in the pictures, which make them want to read the words. Comics beg for repeated readings and let both emerging and reluctant readers enjoy complex stories with a rich vocabulary. But since comics have their own grammar, here are a few tips for reading them with kids:

**GUIDE YOUNG READERS:** Use your finger to show your place in the text, but keep it at the bottom of the character speaking so it doesn't hide the very important facial expressions.

**HAM IT UP!** Think of the comic book story as a play, and don't hesitate to read with expression and intonation. Assign parts or get kids to supply the sound effects, a great way to reinforce phonics skills.

**LET THEM GUESS:** Comics provide lots of context for the words, so emerging readers can make informed guesses. Like jigsaw puzzles, comics ask readers to make connections, so check children's understanding by asking, "What's this character thinking?" (But don't be surprised if a kid finds some of the comics' subtle details faster than you.)

**TALK ABOUT THE PICTURES:** Point out how the artist paces the story with pauses (silent panels) or speeded-up action (a burst of short panels). Discuss how the size and shape of the panels convey meaning.

**ABOVE ALL, ENJOY!** There is of course never one right way to read, so go for the shared pleasure. Once children make the story happen in their imagination, they have discovered the thrill of reading, and you won't be able to stop them. At that point, just go get them more books, and more comics.

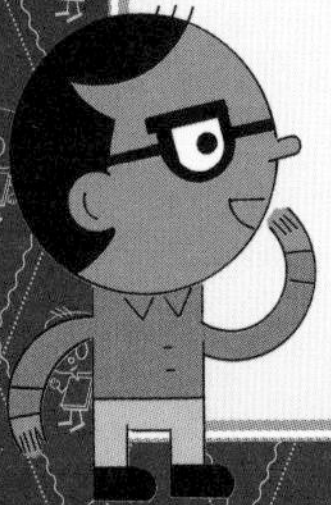

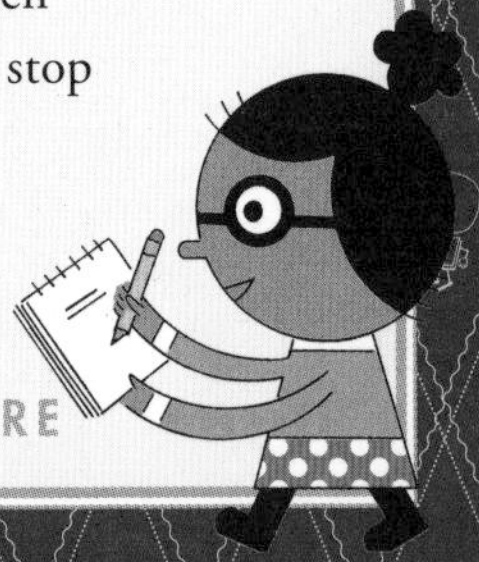

**www.TOON-BOOKS.com**

SEE OUR FREE ONLINE CARTOON MAKERS, LESSON PLANS, AND MUCH MORE